CHASING PERFECTION

CLUB PRIVÉ 3

M. S. PARKER

BELMONTE PUBLISHING, LLC

Copyright © 2016 Belmonte Publishing LLC

Published by Belmonte Publishing LLC

READING ORDER

Thank you so much for reading the Club Privé series. If you'd like to read the complete series, I recommend reading them in this order:

ONE

DEVON

As I used the expensive linen napkin to wipe the wine from my face, I was glad I'd ordered white instead of red. My dry cleaner would be able to salvage my dress shirt. I was still pissed, though. A perfectly good glass of Chardonnay wasted in a fit of childish temper.

"You're breaking up with me?" The beautiful blonde who was still in the midst of the previously mentioned temper tantrum had pushed back from the table and was now standing to deliver her indignant monologue. "Are you fucking kidding me?"

I opened my mouth to tell her to sit down and be quiet, but she didn't let me speak.

"After everything I've let you do to me?" Her face was starting to get that red, splotchy look that happened when fair-skinned women let their temper get the best of them. She looked around at the other diners, most of whom were no longer even trying to be polite and ignore the scene.

"I let you tie me up for your little games!" She was almost shrieking now. "You fucking *spanked* me!"

Shit.

I could see the expressions on the other men and women, saw their eyes darting towards me. Some of them recognized me. That was not acceptable.

I stood and crossed to her in two long strides, putting just an inch between our bodies so we weren't touching, but she was forced to look up at me. I glared down at her and spoke in a low voice, the one that demanded submission.

"You are behaving in a manner most unbecoming, Miss Paine." As it always did when I was trying to control my temper, the faint accent that usually tinged my words thickened until I sounded more like the teenaged boy who'd first stepped off the plane from Venice. That just made me angrier. My next statement was nearly a growl. "You know what happens when you misbehave in public."

Her mouth snapped shut.

I watched her swallow hard and the anger in her face drained away, replaced by lust. I preferred that look on a woman's face. Lust was easy to control.

I took a step back and motioned for one of the waiters who'd been nervously standing in the shadows.

"Yes, Sir?" the man asked nervously.

"Bill me for the meal," I said. "And a bottle of wine for each table as an apology for the disruption of your guests' meals." I glanced at the waiter. "And add a thirty percent tip for your aggravation as well."

"Thank you, Sir."

I turned my attention back to my soon-to-be former lover. "Follow me."

I didn't bother to check if she was following as I walked towards the exit. I kept my eyes forward, my head up, expression blank. The only thing that betrayed what was bubbling under the surface was my lips pressed in a thin line. I stepped out into the balmy autumn night, not pausing to see if she was coming. I walked around the corner and into the narrow alley that separated the expensive Beverly Hills restaurant from the boutique next door. Less than a minute later, she appeared, stepping into the alley without a moment of hesitation.

"Face the wall, palms flat against it."

I could see her fingers trembling as she did as she was told. She knew what was coming, and the fact that she was here meant that she accepted it, wanted it. She was always free to walk away at any time. I knew she wouldn't, though. They never did.

I closed the space between us and slid my hands under the hem of her shirt. I had instructed her to wear the two-piece dress combination rather than a full dress for just this reason. Of all my lovers, Sami had been one of the most contentious – and not always in an enjoyable way – requiring far more discipline than the others. It hadn't been a difficult decision to end our... encounter.

I pulled down her skirt and tapped her bare calf. She lifted one leg, then the other, kicking away half of the twenty-five hundred dollar garment. The top came down to the middle of her ass, leaving the rest of her bare. Like all my women, she didn't wear panties in public. I preferred easy access at all times. I only allowed those who needed it to wear a bra. Sami didn't.

I wasn't interested in her breasts at the moment, however. I ran my hand over the firm globes of pale flesh and felt her tense. I smiled and drew my hand back.

The first crack echoed in the alley, sounding louder because of the silence between us. She didn't make a sound until my hand made contact for the third time, the skin on her ass already starting to turn a delightful shade of pink.

"Ahhh..." It wasn't exactly pleasure, but it wasn't pain either. Sami was in that place where the two were starting to join, but her body hadn't sorted out how it wanted to respond.

I spanked her harder, reminding her that this was a punishment for her behavior. It wasn't meant to truly hurt her, but she needed to feel it. My palm was starting to sting and I was starting to wish I'd thought to bring a belt. Used correctly, it worked as well as a flogger to bring my submissive right to that edge.

I didn't stop until her breathing began to hitch and I could see the moisture between her legs. Only then did I reach into my pocket for one of the little packets I kept on me at all times. I tore it open, unzipped my pants and rolled the condom down over my throbbing cock.

When I stepped up behind her and nudged her legs further apart, I could feel the heat radiating off of her ass. She wasn't going to be able to sit comfortably for days. I lined myself up and thrust into her pussy with one hard stroke.

She keened as I buried my full length inside her. She was wet, but still so tight that it was almost painful for me, but I didn't stop. I grabbed a handful of her hair as I began to pound into her. I could feel her body quivering around me as I tugged on her hair. For as much as she'd made it sound like I was the one who wanted it rough, she got off on it just as much as I did.

I could feel the pressure building in my stomach and knew I was close. I'd been wound too tight from the moment she'd started her tantrum, and spanking her had just made it that much worse. I put my mouth against her ear.

"Come if you can, but I'm not helping you."

She growled in frustration, but I ignored her. My own release was too near. I lowered my head to the place where her shoulder met her neck and took some of the skin there into my mouth, sucking on it, nibbling it with my teeth. We were done, but I'd make sure she'd remember our last time together.

She was making whining little mews now, pushing back to meet my thrusts, forcing me even deeper. I put my hands on her hips and held her in place as I slammed into her, biting down on her neck as I came. She wailed, her body shaking around mine, further proof that I wasn't the only one who liked what I'd done.

I closed my eyes for a moment, letting the waves of pleasure wash over and through me. I let out a breath and took a step back, hearing her hiss as I slid out of her. She staggered, as if her legs couldn't hold her, and then rolled so that her back was against the wall, propping her up. She gave me a cat-ate-the-canary kind of smile.

I discarded the condom and tucked myself back into my pants. I pulled out my wallet and withdrew a twenty. "Here." I tossed it towards her. "Take a cab."

I saw the shock settle over her and resisted the urge to roll my eyes. Had she really thought this meant we weren't done?

"Danny will be your agent from here on out. I don't want to see your face again." I turned and started towards the street where my car would be waiting.

I'd just reached the sidewalk when she screamed out, "Asshole!"

I didn't acknowledge it as I thanked the valet, tipped him, and climbed into the driver's seat. Sami was right. I was an asshole, but that's the way it had to be. Two weeks was my usual, four at the max. No attachments. Ever.

Besides, I reasoned as I started towards home, Sami was just another no-talent, wanna-be actress, anyway. The best she could ever hope for would be bit parts in cheap, made-for-TV movies before she made the inevitable transition to adult films. She'd do okay there. She had a nice body and was a decent enough lay, though not as good as she seemed to think she was.

Women like her were a dime a dozen. They all came to Hollywood with the same idea, that their pretty face and tight pussies would let them sleep their way to the top. And I was the top. I was DeVon fucking Ricci, one of the biggest agents in Hollywood. Nothing could touch me.

TWO

KRISSY

I leaned against the edge of my best friend's desk, watching as she put the last of her things into a plastic container. Leave it to Carrie to be overly organized. We were complete opposites that way and I knew my disorganization annoyed her as much as her tidiness annoyed me.

Damn, I was going to miss her.

Carrie Summers had been my best friend since we'd met at Columbia six years ago. We'd been roommates in the dorm, then moved into an apartment after we'd been hired at Webster and Steinberg. We'd met Dena and Leslie here, and the four of us were close, but Carrie and I were closer. Sometimes, I thought that we were more like sisters than friends, and I knew she felt the same way.

"I can't believe we're having cake again." I sighed, putting a bit of drama into it. "It's only been two months since we had cake for your graduation party." I gave her a shrewd look. "You just wanted to feed that sweet tooth, didn't you?"

Carrie gave me a soft smile, the same smile that she'd been

wearing since she'd started making these plans. I loved Carrie, but she'd always been a bit uptight. She'd always been the one who'd needed coaxing to follow her heart and her dreams. Now, she was leaving one of the largest divorce law firms in New York to start her own pro bono law practice helping people who'd been abused, specifically focusing on the sex trafficking industry.

"I'm going to miss you," I said. As soon as I said the words, I wished I could take them back. They hadn't come out as light-hearted as I'd intended, and sincere emotions weren't something I liked showing in public.

Carrie paused in her packing and looked up, giving me a puzzled look. I had to drop my gaze down to where my fingers were tapping at the edge of the desk. I couldn't meet those dark eyes. Not when it was finally time to tell her.

"What do you mean you're going to miss me?" she asked. "I'm only going to be four blocks away. We can still have lunch together every day and meet after work for drinks whenever you want. That's the joy of being my own boss. Flexibility."

I pushed back my thick, glossy black hair. It was past my shoulders now and I was thinking it might be a good idea to cut it before I left. There was a big difference in the weather from here to where I was going.

"Is this about me moving in with Gavin?"

Carrie's question made me look up, startled. I hadn't thought she'd take it that way.

"I thought you said you were okay with it."

I straightened. "I am," I assured her. "I am. Gavin's smoking hot, and a really good guy. I'm glad that you're moving in together."

I was telling the truth. For a while after they'd first met, my approval of Gavin had fluctuated, but once the whole truth had come out, I'd been more than happy to put my stamp of approval on their relationship. Some people might've thought they were moving too fast, but I knew Carrie. She never would've made this decision if she wasn't sure about him, and I'd given her my full support. She deserved to be happy, and so did he.

Carrie folded her arms over her chest and her eyes narrowed. "Well, something's weird with you. What is it, girl? Spill."

Dammit. Why did she always have to be so insightful when it came to me? I'd wanted to ease into this, but like most of my life, I'd fallen into it. "I'm probably leaving the company, too," I said slowly. Carrie's eyes widened. "And that's not all," I continued. "I'm most likely leaving New York as well."

Carrie's jaw dropped and she stared at me for nearly a full, uncomfortable minute. Then her mouth snapped shut and she gave me a suspicious look. "Are you saying this because I'm moving out? If you don't want me to go or you think I'm moving too fast with Gavin, just say so. He'll understand if I change my mind."

Was she serious? I rolled my eyes. "Really, Carrie? Come on. You know me better than that," I said. "I think you and Gavin should definitely move in together. The truth is, there's a job as an associate looking my way."

I saw shock, then hurt, cross her face.

"You've been keeping this a secret from me for how long? Why?"

"I applied three months ago," I said. "And then I had the phone interview two weeks after that. Understand why I didn't say anything?" I saw her doing the math in her head and then watched her frustration with me fade away as she realized that I hadn't told her because she'd had enough going on at the time. "I haven't exactly gotten it yet. Besides, I didn't even know if I'd get called out for a face-to-face interview."

"And that's what this is? Not a definite, but an interview?"

I nodded. "They said it was down to just three applicants now. I think I have a good shot." I paused, then added, "And even if I don't get it, I might look out there anyway."

"Out there?" Carrie echoed. I knew she was still putting the pieces together and had just understood that when I said out of the city, I hadn't meant Jersey. "Where's the job?"

Here was the part I really hadn't been looking forward to. "On the West Coast."

Carrie took a slow, deep breath, letting it out before she asked her next question. "You mean you might move to San Francisco or some place like that?"

"Not San Francisco," I said. "Hollywood."

"Are you nuts? You want to go be some divorce lawyer in L.A.?"

I shook my head. If she hated that idea, she was really going to hate this one. "The offer's from a talent agency."

She frowned. "A talent agency? What, are you trying to become an actress or something?"

It was a mark of our friendship that I took pride in her snide remark. I found it comforting that I'd rubbed off on her over the years. "No, smart-ass," I said. "One of the biggest talent agencies in Hollywood needs another associate in their legal department. Remember that guy, Kenny, who used to work here?"

"The one you made out with in the elevator and then bragged about it over drinks?" Carrie's lips twitched into a grin. "Yeah, I have a vague recollection of him."

I laughed. Even with as kinky as she and Gavin had gotten, Carrie was still hesitant to talk about sex anywhere that wasn't our apartment. Or, based on what I'd heard through our thin walls, the bedroom. "We did a little more than make out, but yes, that's the one. He's been trying to get back in my pants ever since. His cousin works at the agency and told him they were looking for another associate. He figured it'd be a good reason to call."

"Did you go out with him again?" Carried asked.

I shook my head. "No way. He wasn't that good, or that hot." I ignored the judgey look she was sending my way. She might keep her mouth shut about it most of the time, but I knew she didn't approve of the way I handled my romantic life. "But I did decide to send in my résumé and now they want me to fly in for an interview."

"When are you leaving?"

"Monday morning. The meeting's at noon."

"I'm happy you have this opportunity," Carrie said. Her eyes were bright with tears. "But if you get this job, am I ever going to see you again, or is this it?"

I rolled my eyes again. "Of course we'll see each other." I playfully pushed at her arm, trying to lighten the mood. This is exactly what I hadn't wanted. "I'll come visit. Or, here's an idea. You and Gavin can move to LA. Start your little sexy club out there. Give me a good place to scope out all those California hotties."

"Krissy." Carrie said my name with a combination of affection and irritation.

"And your pro bono business can be just as effective on the West Coast. There are plenty of young women being abused in California. Trust me. Probably more than in New York."

Carrie frowned. "That's not funny."

I held up my hands in a gesture of surrender. I knew I'd crossed the line as soon as the words had left my mouth. "I know, I know. Crude," I said. "But I'm pretty sure that's a true statement."

Carrie nodded, and her expression shifted to one of sadness. "What am I going to do without you?"

I put my arm around her shoulders. If she started crying, I was going to start and I didn't particularly like the idea of walking around for the next hour or so with red eyes.

"Come on," I said. "Let's go get some of that cake. I heard Mimi ordered the same as last time: Red Velvet with cream cheese frosting."

Carrie gave a laugh that had a sniffle in the middle of it. "She *always* orders Red Velvet..."

I laughed and started to walk us both towards the conference room. I hadn't told Mimi about the interview yet. That was another conversation I didn't really want to have. I pushed down the butterflies that wanted to make an appearance. I wasn't usually the nervous type, but even I had a bit of anxiety about this one. It would be my first big venture completely on my own. Going away to college didn't really count. This was the first adult move I'd be making, and it would be across the country, all by myself. On the one hand, I was excited by the prospect of a change, of soaking up the sun in LA, rubbing elbows with all of the beautiful people; but on the other hand, I'd miss all of my friends. No matter what I told Carrie, I wasn't sure how often I'd be able to make it back across the country. I didn't want to lose the people I cared about, but I didn't want to pass up this chance.

I forced thoughts of myself to the back of my mind as Carrie and I entered the conference room. This wasn't the time or place. This was Carrie's moment to say her good-byes and get her well wishes. My time was coming.

THREE

KRISSY

I'd flown before, but I'd never been so thankful to have my feet firmly on the ground. I carefully made my way through the corridor, walking more steadily than some of my fellow passengers, most of whom looked just as green as I felt. Despite the anxiety and nausea caused by our turbulent six-hour flight, I also saw smiles on many of the faces as we stepped into the LAX terminal.

I stopped as I stepped into a patch of sunlight. I tilted my head back and closed my eyes, letting myself soak it in. I'd left a cloudy and overcast New York at seven thirty in the morning and arrived in sunny Los Angeles at ten thirty, thanks to the time zone changes. I had thirty minutes before my interview, so I headed to the bathrooms first to freshen up. My phone said only three hours had passed, but I probably looked like the full six the trip had taken.

Not even that thought could take the smile off of my face. My queasiness had settled, proving that it had only been the turbulence and not nerves. Now I was ready. Not just ready. I was excited.

I was here. Los Angeles. The City of Dreams. This was the

only place in the world where your handyman would give you his screenplay after fixing your air conditioner. In New York, there were the waiters and waitresses who were waiting for their big break on Broadway or as 'serious' writers, but in Hollywood, pretty much everyone wanted to be something more.

I had only my carry-on with me since I was only staying for a couple of days, which meant I didn't have to stop at the baggage claim. That was good. I wanted to have the time to make myself look presentable. No, I amended. I wanted to look good. I stepped into the bathroom, put my bag on the counter and got to work. The company had offered to put me up in a hotel for two nights so that if they wanted a second interview, I wouldn't have to fly back out in two days. They'd been very accommodating.

When I was sure that my tanned skin looked flawless and my thick black hair was behaving itself, I smoothed down the skirt of my sensible business suit and headed back out into the main lobby. This time, I went for the line of people waiting for pick-ups. Sure enough, there was a man in a black suit holding a sign with my name on it. I grinned when I saw that they'd actually spelled it right. Points to Mirage Talent. I don't know how many job offers I'd turned down because they spelled my name wrong or tried to make it Kristine or Kristen. Nope. It was just Krissy, and if they couldn't take the time to learn that, I didn't want to work for them.

"Ms. Jensen." The driver inclined his head as I approached. "May I take your bag?"

A slightly snarky and very inappropriate comment popped into my head, but I held my tongue. Even if the driver was kinda cute in a tall and gawky kind of way, I wasn't going to risk a potentially awesome job for a one-liner.

"Thank you," I said as I handed over the bag. It wasn't very heavy, but it was on the bulky side, so carrying it always made me feel like I was walking lopsided, especially in the four inch heels I'd chosen for today.

I was a little over average height even without the shoes, and they put me a nice five foot ten. That was a good height, I'd found, for meeting new clients and potential employers. Tall enough so that I didn't have to strain to talk to taller men, but not so tall that I ended up towering over most of them. I'd also found that the heels complemented my figure. I was just a touch too curvy to be considered slender, but the heels made my legs look longer and thinner.

I felt good as I followed the driver to a black Town Car. I'd felt the admiring looks from men, and a couple women, as I'd passed and knew that I'd chosen the right ensemble for the day. I wanted admiration, not cat calls. Attractive but professional was always the right call for first impressions. If I got the job, I'd take a lay of the land and figure out where I was on the fashion scale.

The driver didn't say a word as he eased into the infamous LA traffic and began to make his way towards Mirage Talent. I stared out the tinted windows, completely enchanted by the skyline. It was so different than New York or Chicago. The sky seemed so much bigger here, the sun brighter. I hadn't realized just how much I was going to love it. I'd told Carrie that I might look around for another job out here if I didn't get the one at Mirage, but I'd only been half-serious. Now, after less than half an hour in California, I was certain this was where I wanted to be.

The car pulled up in front of an impressive building with the Mirage logo on the front of its steel and glass exterior. I took a deep breath, feeling a small flutter of nerves in my stomach. I had to admit, the place was a little intimidating.

"My bag?" I asked the driver as he opened the door.

"I'll be the one taking you to your hotel, Miss, so the bag is safe in the trunk." His face was carefully blank, the kind of professional expression that told me, despite his youthful appearance, he'd been doing this for a while.

"Thank you," I said as I started towards the front doors.

It took all of my self-control not to gawk at the lobby as I walked inside. It was done in the same steel and glass style as the exterior, but inside it was even more impressive. People expected the outsides of buildings to be like that, but the inside made it feel like something sleek and modern. It was the exact opposite of the old-fashioned antiques and art work of Webster and Steinberg. I'd never been very fond of that style. This, however, this I liked. I could work here and love every minute of being in this building.

The receptionist beamed at me as I approached and I wondered if she was really that friendly or if it was an act. If I was back in New York, I would've leaned towards fake, but she seemed genuine.

"Hi." I returned her smile with one of my own. No way was I going to get the reputation as the bitchy New Yorker. "I'm here for an appointment. Krissy Jensen."

"Of course, Miss Jensen," she said. "If you just keep going through that set of doors, you'll come to the reception seating area. Have a seat in there and you'll be called as soon as they're ready for you."

The seating area was just as gorgeous as the lobby. Across from the set of doors I'd just come through were two more doors, also steel and glass, but these were frosted so that I couldn't see what lay behind them. To my left was a huge leather couch and, across from it, separated by a massive glass coffee table, were two large leather chairs.

A handsome young man was already sitting in one of the chairs, so I headed for the couch. I picked up a magazine off of table and opened it without really looking at it. I stole a glance at the man across from me, and then took a second look. He had the white blond hair, blue eyes and tan that I'd always associated with California guys, the kind of guy who looked like he'd be just at home on a beach, wearing shorts and carrying a surfboard, as he was sitting across from me in khakis and a button-down shirt.

"Who's your agent?"

It took me a moment to realize that he was talking to me.

"Oh, I'm not here for...I'm an attorney." I smiled at him. "I'm here for a job interview."

"Ah." His teeth flashed white against his tanned skin and I wondered how often he had to bleach them. No one had teeth that white.

"I'm Krissy Jensen," I said.

"Taylor Moore." He leaned across the table and held out a hand.

I took it, giving him a firm and brief handshake. Normally, I would've been all over that, but I didn't think it was smart to hit on a client, or at least someone who was the client of my potential employer.

"You know," he said as he leaned back. "I have to admit, I wouldn't have pegged you for a lawyer."

I raised an eyebrow. If he was going to flirt, I wasn't going to encourage him, but I wasn't going to say no, either.

His grin widened, showing dimples. "Women in LA who look like you are models or actresses." His gaze ran over me, the light in his eyes saying that he was definitely being more than polite. "I'm guessing you're under five eight, so probably not a model, even though you're gorgeous enough to be one."

He got points for saying I was too short, not that I was too...curvaceous.

"So I guessed an actress."

"Wrong, but very observant," I said as I set aside my magazine.

"And you're not from around here," he commented. "I thought I'd caught an accent before. Now I'm sure. Where are you from?"

"New..." I paused. "Born and raised in Chicago, but I've been in New York for a while."

He nodded. "I'm from Wisconsin." When I didn't pry with a question, he offered more information. "I came out here after high school to be an actor. I've done a few commercials. Local stuff, so you wouldn't have seen me in anything...yet. I've got things in the works. Who are you interviewing with?"

I had to admit, I was impressed. He was definitely into me, but he hadn't asked yet if I was married or had a boyfriend. Most guys would've asked that question first or second, not wanting to waste their time with someone who was already taken.

"The head of the legal department. Mr. Duncan."

He nodded. "That's good. It's a good thing it's not with DeVon."

That didn't sound good. I knew DeVon Ricci was the head of the company, but I hadn't done a lot of research on him. I'd focused on Duncan, since that's who I had to get through first. If I made it to the second interview, then I'd planned to start looking into Ricci. Now I wasn't so sure I'd made the right choice. Maybe I should've checked Ricci out first.

"What's wrong with Mr. Ricci?"

Taylor shrugged. "Let's say DeVon has his own...unique style." He sounded like he was being very careful with his word choices. "If you were interviewing with DeVon, I think he'd scare you off and I want you to stick around."

I gave him a polite smile. "Thank you." I straightened. "But I wouldn't be too worried," I added. "I don't scare easily."

"Miss Jensen?" A petite red-head came through the frosted glass doors. "Mr. Duncan will see you now."

I stood and smoothed down my skirt. "It was nice to have met you."

"And you," Taylor said. His eyes ran down my legs. "I look forward to seeing more of you very soon."

The heat in his eyes suggested he wasn't just talking about seeing me again around the agency. When he said more, he meant *more* and it took all of my self-control not to fire back with a double-entendre of my own.

"Have a good day," I said as I followed the red-head through the doors. I could feel Taylor's eyes on me as I walked. I was pretty sure he was staring at my ass, so I put a little more swing in my hips than I normally would have. Might as well leave him with a good impression.

I was definitely liking Hollywood.

"Mr. Duncan?" The red-head knocked on an open door at the end of a corridor.

I caught a glimpse of an elevator to my left. A sign next to it said "Private." That must lead to the mysterious Mr. Ricci, I thought as I walked into the office.

An attractive man in his mid-fifties stood on the other side of a very expensive-looking desk. He had such light-colored hair that, at first, I wasn't sure if it was blond or white, but then I realized that he had been blond, but his hair was streaked with silver, giving it a strange, dual-colored look. His eyes were intelligent and a pale gray that contrasted strongly with his tanned skin. My boss back home would've been all over this guy.

"Mr. Duncan." I gave him my best professional smile as I held out my hand.

His handshake was brisk, but not rude. That was good. Too many men either snatched their hands away like they were afraid I'd read something into their touch if they lingered too long, or they purposefully lingered, turning the shake into a holding.

"Please, have a seat." He gestured to the chair across from his.

I sat carefully, crossing my ankles and tucking my feet under my chair. My skirt was an appropriate length for work, but I didn't want to take any chances on flashing my prospective boss. He didn't seem like the type who'd appreciate the view. And I was grateful for that. I didn't want someone more interested in what was between my legs than what was between my ears.

"You have quite an impressive résumé for someone so young, Miss Jensen," he began.

The interview was like something out of a dream. He asked specific questions and seemed pleased with the answers I gave, though not overly exuberant about them. Another good sign. He wanted to make sure I knew that I'd done well, but didn't want to show any sort of sign as to how I measured up against the competition.

"I do have to ask, Miss Jensen," Mr. Duncan said as he set

down my résumé. "Do you have any desire to become an actress, model or celebrity of any kind?"

The question surprised me, but I didn't let it show. "No, Sir," I answered promptly. "I've never wanted to be in the spotlight like that. Put me in a courtroom in front of a judge and jury, and I'll be a star, but I don't want to be in front of a camera."

He gave me a partial smile. "That's very good, Miss Jensen. You understand, in our business, we get a lot of attractive young people who see this place as a stepping stone, but not to rise in the legal department. They think that they can use us to get their 'big break' and that is not something we encourage."

"I understand." I nodded, thankful that I was being completely honest. "I'm not interested in any of that. I want to rise in the company, but as a lawyer, not as anything else." I decided that bold was a good idea. "In fact, Sir, I'd like to see myself sitting in that desk one day." I let one side of my mouth twitch up into a half smile. "Many years from now, of course."

Mr. Duncan gave me a full smile, his eyes twinkling. It was good to know that the serious face wasn't all there was to him. "That's very good, Miss Jensen." He stood and I did the same. "While we do have other interviews to conduct, I would like you to come in tomorrow for a second interview."

I tried not to let how excited I was show. "Thank you, Sir."

"And, Miss Jensen," he added. "You are one of our most promising candidates."

Now I couldn't stop the smile. "Thank you." I almost sounded like I was gushing and I forced myself to rein it in.

"Your driver will take you to your hotel. Enjoy the rest of your day here and be back at nine tomorrow morning, prepared for a more in-depth interview. We are only conducting two second interviews, so it is imperative that you come fully prepared."

I wasn't sure, but that sounded to me like a warning. Taylor's comment about DeVon Ricci came back to me. As I walked out of the office, I wondered if that's what Mr. Duncan had meant. Was I going to be meeting the big boss tomorrow? And if I was, what could he possibly have planned that I would need to prepare for? I had to admit, the thought did make me a little nervous.

I set my jaw as I walked back out into the California sun. I wasn't going to let it bother me. I knew I was perfect for this job and nothing was going to keep me from making sure everyone at Mirage Talent knew it too.

FOUR

KRISSY

I had a feeling my driver was taking the scenic route to the hotel. I wasn't minding, though. I'd never seen anything like this city before and even my excitement over how well the interview had gone couldn't distract me from the view. When we finally pulled up in front of the hotel, I was eager to get to my room, shower and head out into the sunshine. I hadn't eaten much that morning, not liking to fly on a full stomach, and I was starting to get hungry. I couldn't wait to see what Los Angeles had to offer.

I thanked the driver as he handed my bag to the valet waiting at the entrance. This was a nicer hotel than any I'd been to in New York, but it was impossible to compare them, really. New York was stone and history. No matter how updated their buildings were, they always had a sense of being old, especially the swankiest hotels. This one was modern, with clean-cut lines. If New York was 'old money' then this was new, and I loved it.

"Miss Jensen, you've been upgraded." The clerk at the desk gave me a pleasant smile.

"Excuse me?" I knew I couldn't have heard her correctly.

Mirage was a wealthy company and they obviously liked to show their potential employees a good time, but a hospitality suite at a hotel like this was already above and beyond.

"You've been upgraded to a top floor suite," the woman clarified.

"By whom?" I didn't mean to sound rude, but it was a bit of a shock. I mean, my interview had gone well, but this was ridiculous.

The clerk's smile faltered for a moment, then came back, steady as ever. Definitely a wanna-be actress. "Mirage Talent, of course," she said. She slid a keycard across the desk. "Marcus will help you with your bag."

"That's okay," I said. "I can take it from here." I held out my hand and, after a moment, was handed my bag. I just wanted to be alone to process.

When I got off on the top floor, I still hadn't figured out why I'd been upgraded. Maybe tomorrow was just a formality, I thought. This could be their way of welcoming me to the company. If it was, wow. I smiled. Whatever the reason, I was going to enjoy it.

I took half a dozen steps into the room as the door swung shut behind me, and that's when I realized I wasn't alone.

In the center of the room was a massive couch and my trio of visitors were centered around it. I stared at them for several seconds, unable to believe what I was seeing. Two were women: one a red-head, the other blonde, neither of them naturals. I could tell because, unfortunately, neither of them was clothed. One was on all fours on the couch, her ass towards me as she kissed the man sitting on the couch. The other woman was kneeling between his legs, running her hands up and down his thighs. He, at least, appeared to be clothed. Not that it made things better, because while he was kissing the red-head, he had one hand between her legs, two long fingers sliding into her. His other hand was on the blonde's breast, pinching and twisting one rose-colored nipple.

I processed all of this in the time it took for me to regain my voice and to overcome my shock.

"Excuse me." My voice came out stronger than I'd expected. "What are you doing in my room?" And, as I always did when I was mostly at a loss for words, I said exactly what I was thinking, no matter if it was appropriate or not. "Are you having some kind of orgy in my hotel room?"

The man on the couch rolled the red-head onto her back so that she was lying across his lap, her legs spread so that I could see more than I wanted to. His fingers slid back inside her and she moaned, writhing on his lap.

"What else would it be?" The man had a faint accent; Italian, I thought. "Come join us."

I looked at him now, my temper flaring. Who the hell did he think he was? "Join you? No fucking way." I sneered at him. "You couldn't handle me."

I let my eyes rake over him, taking in the wild black waves of hair that fell across his forehead, the rich brown eyes. He was handsome, with strong features rather than the pretty-boy look Taylor had going on. His shirt was unbuttoned, revealing a firm, defined chest. He was lean but his body was cut in a way that would usually make me wet. The fact that he was still fingering the red-head and the blonde was crawling up next to him, her large breasts swaying as she moved...that all kinda pissed me off, so arousal wasn't exactly my emotion at the moment.

"Get the fuck out of my room before I call security." I gave the women my most derisive glare. "And take your bimbos with you."

His eyes flashed, but the corners of his mouth twitched like he was amused by something. When he spoke, however, his voice was flat. "You don't know who you're talking to, do you?"

"Yeah," I retorted. "An asshole."

He laughed, sliding his fingers out of the red-head's pussy. He held his hand out to the blonde, barely glancing at her as she began to lick his fingers clean. The red-head made a protesting sound, but he ignored her, too. "I like your smart mouth," he said. "Duncan will definitely be pleased with you."

I frowned. Duncan? He couldn't mean Leon Duncan, the head of the legal department at Mirage Talent, the man I'd just interviewed with.

"Oh, that's right. We were never properly introduced." He stood, spilling the women off of his lap.

I couldn't stop my eyes from flicking down over his torso to his narrow waist, my curiosity getting the better of me. I tried very hard not to lick my lips at the impressive bulge at the front of his tailored, gray slacks.

"Krissy."

My name brought my attention back up with a snap. I could feel heat creeping up my cheeks.

"I'm DeVon Ricci. Your new boss."

My stomach plummeted. Fuck. What kind of shit-storm did I just walk into? I shook my head, refusing to believe it. "I never met DeVon Ricci. How do you know who I am?"

He grinned and held out his hand. The hand that had been between the red-head's legs. No way in hell was I going to shake that. I folded my arms across my chest. He dropped his hand and used it to gesture towards the coffee table in front of the couch.

"I was watching your interview. Duncan has a webcam on his computer that allows me to watch all of his interviews. I find it saves time weeding out the candidates."

"So, what is this, then?" My hands curled into fists, my fingernails digging into my palms. "I join in the fun and I get the job?"

He raised an eyebrow, a gesture that usually went straight through me. I wasn't going to let this one do that. I focused on how pissed I was.

"Well," he said. "I never give out guarantees." He ran his gaze down my body in that slow way that said he was imagining how I looked naked. "But it might put you at the front of the line." His eyes were darker as they met mine, and I knew he'd liked what I saw. "That is how my last assistant got hired."

His voice was dripping sex, promising pleasure I couldn't imagine. Damn, he was hot. I shifted my weight from one foot to the other. Too bad he was a complete tool. There was no way in hell I was joining in. "Like I said." My voice was even, but I could hear the fury in every word. "This is my room, so I'll give you and your bimbos thirty second to get the fuck out before I call security. I have another important interview tomorrow and I'd like to relax."

DeVon's eyes narrowed as he studied me for a moment and I held his gaze. I had nothing to be ashamed of here and I wasn't going to look away first. Finally, he glanced over his shoulder and held out his hands. "Ladies."

The women stood, bending over to pick up what I assumed were their clothes. They pulled skimpy dresses over their heads, not bothering with any undergarments. I really hoped that was because they hadn't been wearing any. I didn't want to sit down and find a pair of panties under the cushions. I glanced at the couch. On second thought, I'd just sit in one of the chairs.

DeVon let the women leave first and then he paused, turning back towards me.

"Congratulations, Miss Jensen." His tone was serious now, no hint of flirtation. "If you had joined us, you wouldn't be getting to stay here in this lovely suite preparing for your interview tomorrow. You would be on your way back to New York. Mirage Talent does not hire women who use sex to get ahead."

I gaped at him. Seriously? The whole thing had been a set-up? I wasn't sure if I should be relieved, horrified or even more furious. I chose the latter. I scowled. "I thought you said that's how your last assistant got hired."

A glint appeared in his eyes and one side of his mouth tipped up, giving me that sexual smile again. "There is always the exception to the rule." He stepped into the hallway, getting the last word in as the door closed. "She was fucking hot."

FIVE

DEVON

The thing I hated the most about what I'd done was the fact that I'd had to carry my jacket in front of me while I waited for my hard-on to go down. I was glad Krissy Jensen had turned me down – my lips twitched at the memory of how pissed she'd been – but it definitely made for an uncomfortable ride back to the office.

I was still thinking about the way her dark eyes had flashed when Leon Duncan stepped out of his office before I could get on to the private elevator to my office. I was turned towards him when something flew through the air, narrowly missing my face.

"You bastard." Leon's face was red. "You were spying on me!"

Sometimes, I wondered if complete honesty was always worth the trouble. I looked down to see the webcam I'd had installed shattered at my feet. I looked back up at the head of my legal department and spoke in a cool, even tone despite feeling anything but cool.

"You will do well to remember that I am your employer, and calm the hell down." I waited for a moment to see how he responded. As I'd hoped he would, he took a slow breath and some of the color receded from his face. "If you look over the contract you signed – and you wrote, may I remind you – there is an entire section that states all company property may be monitored at any time at my discretion."

"I-I thought that was to keep people from surfing for porn or making personal calls on company time." Leon was flustered, but I didn't know if it was because he'd just realized that he'd thrown something at his boss, or because I was right and he had no legal standing to be mad.

"That is the main reason," I admitted. "But it allowed me to monitor the interviews." I paused, then added, "And that's all I monitored. I wasn't spying on you, Leon. I wanted to see the remaining candidates before they did their interview with me."

Now he just looked puzzled. The man was great at the legal stuff, but he wasn't a businessman. His brain just didn't work that way.

"Why?" Leon asked. "Whoever I hire isn't going to be working directly under you. She'll be in my department. You've never been interested in who I hired before."

"This time, it's different," I said. I didn't have to explain myself, but Leon was a good man. When he wasn't throwing expensive electrical equipment at my head. I wanted him to understand. "I don't want to keep thinking so narrowly. There could be potential among these candidates. Maybe someone who could rise above just being a lawyer sitting behind a desk."

Leon raised an eyebrow. "Like who?"

"Krissy Jensen," I answered immediately. She'd been the only one who'd struck me as anything special. "There's something about her." *Something more than a tight ass and nice tits*, I wanted to add, but that wouldn't have been appropriate.

Leon shook his head. "Jensen, really? She's good, I'll give you that. And I like her attitude, but Melissa Tomes is much better qualified. I'd put Ms. Jensen as a runner-up, but Ms. Tomes scored higher on every test. She has to be first choice."

I had crossed the distance between us before I'd realized what I was doing and it was all I could do not to grab the front of his shirt and yank him up onto his tiptoes. That would've been a bit extreme, I thought.

I spoke slowly and clearly so that he would understand me. "It's not about test scores or experience. Someone could look good on paper, but be as exciting as a pile of dog shit. In fact, that is your first choice. Melissa is books and ass-kissing. We work with people and we need to hire people with skills in that field. Someone with fire in their veins and steel in their backbone. *That* is what Krissy Jensen brings."

I turned and walked back to the elevator, catching a glimpse of Leon's face, pale and mottled with pink from the sudden change from anger to intimidated. My entire body was thrumming with energy as I got onto the elevator. Maybe I should have gone to the gym, I thought. I was way too tense. I should've known better, getting wound up like that without any release.

I was two steps into my office when I realized that I wasn't alone.

Cheri was leaning against my desk, completely naked. The skimpy dress she'd worn out of the hotel was lying in a chair.

"What the fuck are you doing here?" I snapped. "How did you get here before me?" I looked around, fully expecting a blonde to appear. "Where's Tina?"

Cheri grinned at me as she ran a hand over one pert breast, cupping the firm flesh. "She had to leave to see her dentist or something, but I snuck in while you were talking with Duncan. You really should get better security."

"I'll keep that in mind," I spoke through gritted teeth. I was pissed, but I couldn't quit looking at her fingers playing with her nipple.

"Do you mind that I came to see you?" She pushed herself off of the desk and walked towards me.

"Yes, I fucking mind! Get the hell out!"

Cheri's smile widened as she leaned against me. I should have taken a step back, but I could feel the heat of her blazing through my clothes and all of the pent-up tension I had from the hotel came rushing back. Never one for subtly, she ran her hand over my crotch and my blood went straight south.

"You seem tense," she teased. "Do you need a massage?" Her hand slowly rubbed the bulge in my pants.

I closed my eyes and clenched my hands into fists. I could feel myself swelling under her hand. "Fuck," I muttered.

Then her hand was gone and I opened my eyes. I wasn't sure if I wanted her to have left or still be there, offering herself to me. I was strung so tight that I wasn't entirely sure I could remember my name. If she'd left, I'd have to spend a couple minutes in the bathroom before I'd be any good at work.

She hadn't left. She'd just moved to her knees. When she saw me looking down at her, she reached for my zipper. As she opened my pants, she licked her lips, leaving no doubt as to what she intended to do.

Aw, hell. How was I supposed to say no to that?

I buried my fingers in her hair as she pulled my cock out of my pants. I was so hard it almost hurt, and I knew I wasn't going to last long. Cheri was tall, making access to her mouth easier than it would've been on someone shorter, like Tina.

"Open your mouth," I growled.

She did as she was told. She knew exactly what I wanted. I shoved the first three inches between her lips, groaning as she swirled her tongue around my swollen shaft. There was no way I would last long at all.

"I'm going to fuck your mouth." My accent had thickened as my need grew.

"Please."

Cheri only managed that single word before I was shoving her head down the length of my cock. She'd given me a blow job before so I knew how far she could take me. I took her to that point over and over again, using her hair to pull her off of me before shoving back into that hot, wet cavern. I looked down at Cheri, her mouth stretched wide around me, my cock glistening with her saliva, and suddenly, it wasn't her red hair and porcelain skin I was seeing.

Thick black hair between my fingers.

Large, dark eyes peering up at me from between thick lashes.

Krissy.

My entire body shuddered as I came without warning. I jerked back, the last of my cum splashing across Cheri's face. I stared down at her, my heart pounding in my chest. She grinned at me as she got to her feet, licking her lips and wiping her hand across her face.

"I got no problem swallowing, hun, but warn a girl next time." She chuckled.

What the hell?

"Get out."

Cheri looked startled, but I didn't care. I grabbed her dress from the chair and threw it at her. "Get dressed and get the fuck out!"

She scowled at me as she pulled on her dress, but she didn't argue. I barely even noticed when she closed the door behind her.

What the hell? I sank into my chair, my hands shaking. I never lost control. I WAS control. But something about the thought of having Krissy on her knees, her lips around my cock...

I slapped my hand against my desk, letting the sting clear my head. Whatever it was, it was done, and it wouldn't happen again.

SIX

KRISSY

I was torn between wanting to open the door and throw something at my maybe-future-boss, and getting on a plane to go back home. I didn't do either. Instead, I carried my bag back to the bedroom and then went into the bathroom to clean up. My stomach was growling and a glance at a clock told me it was almost two, which meant five on the East Coast, and I hadn't eaten anything substantial yet today. I needed to get something to eat or I was going to end up with a massive headache.

As I headed down in the elevator, I kept thinking about what had just happened. I knew there were bosses who pressed for sexual favors but I'd never heard of one who wanted to be told no. I supposed it was a good thing and I should be grateful DeVon – Mr. Ricci – hadn't been serious, but I still wasn't sure how I felt about what I'd walked in on. I mean, I was no prude, but that had been...too much.

I shook my head. I didn't want to think about DeVon and his naked women. I had changed out of my interview clothes and into a cute little dress that Carrie's boyfriend, Gavin, had been nice enough to buy for me one of the times I'd taken Carrie shopping. It was a warm, gold color that complemented my skin tone and it accentuated my curves, drawing attention to my narrow waist as much as my bust.

"Hi." I gave the concierge a bright smile. Judging by the expression on his face, I'd chosen the dress well. "I was just wondering if you could recommend a good lunch restaurant."

"Of course."

I was impressed at how well he did not staring at my breasts. I didn't know many men with that much self-control. For a second, I wondered if DeVon would've pretended not to notice, or if he'd openly ogle. I was willing to bet the latter.

"There are several excellent restaurants at Sunset Plaza. Clafoutis is quite well-regarded."

"Thank you," I said. I started to turn away when he spoke again.

"Would you like a complimentary ride?"

Surprised, I nodded. "Thank you. That would be great."

It wasn't until I was in the hotel's town car, heading for Sunset Plaza, that I thought to wonder if this was another test by Mirage, or just something nice the hotel or the company did.

No, I told myself. I wasn't going to second-guess every decision I made, worried about what Mr. Ricci would think. I was going to do what I knew was right and not worry about anything else. I wanted this job and I really wanted to live out here, but I wasn't about to compromise anything I believed. No job was worth that. And accepting a complimentary ride from the hotel was far from unethical.

When we arrived at the Plaza, the driver opened the door for me and asked if I wanted him to wait or if I'd prefer to call the hotel for a pick-up. I chose the call option, not knowing how long I was going to linger over lunch, or if I'd take a walk when I was done. I'd chosen flat sandals rather than heels just for that reason.

Several restaurants sat next to each other, each one looking just as good as the last. I spotted the one the concierge had mentioned and decided to take his advice. It was absolutely gorgeous and had an array of tables out on a patio where I'd be able to enjoy the sunshine and people-watch.

Their menu was amazing. I almost couldn't decide. Finally, I chose the Gazpacho – a seasoned cold tomato soup with garlic croutons – a turkey club with everything on it, and a side of garden vegetables.

As I settled in under the partial shade and began to eat, I watched the beautiful people of Hollywood walk by, sporting the latest fashions, arms linked as they chattered away about the latest gossip. It was nothing like watching New York sidewalks. Everyone there was so busy, hurrying from one place to the next. There was a sameness about them. Not because everyone in New York looked the same, but they all had the same harried expressions, whether they were in a three-piece suit or wearing leather. It was all important business. Here, there was a mixture of those rushing and those taking their time, but even the people in a hurry didn't carry themselves with the same briskness I associated with the people of big cities like Chicago or New York.

Then there was the traffic. I'd heard horror stories about LA traffic, and having lived in the Big Apple, I was no stranger to cars parked bumper to bumper. I didn't know if it was the time of day or where I was, but it wasn't too bad. The main difference between the two cities, however, was the type of car. Back home, every other car would be a yellow taxi. Here, every second or third car cruising by was a Ferrari, Lamborghini, Porsche or another exotic car that cost more than I made in a year. Hell, some of them were worth almost twice as much as I made in a year.

I knew the saying about the grass being greener on the other side of the fence, and I'd worried that I was trying to do that to LA, but that's not what it looked like to me from here. I was sure there'd be disadvantages to living here, just like there were negatives about every place, but sitting there, enjoying the more relaxed atmosphere and the warmth of the sun, I couldn't see it. Being here just made me all the more determined to get hired at Mirage.

"Krissy!"

I blinked, startled out of my reverie by my name being called. From the sound of it, it wasn't the first time. I looked around, trying to figure out who I knew out here who could possibly be yelling for me. I spotted him even as he came towards me. Blond hair, tanned skin and that impossible smile.

"Hello again, Taylor." I returned the smile. He was off-limits for anything sexual or romantic, but a talk wasn't unethical.

"Here I was thinking I'd have to make an excuse to go back to Mirage just so I could see you again." His eyes ran over me and he gave a low whistle. "Much better than what you were wearing before. Not," he hastily added, "that there was anything wrong with you before. It's just that dress..."

"Were you just walking by, or coming to get something to eat?" I asked the first question that popped into my head so he'd quit talking about the way I looked. Normally, I loved a compliment, but I couldn't flirt back. It wouldn't be right, not when I still had a chance at the Mirage job.

"I come here all the time," he explained, his eyes returning to meet mine. "I live two blocks that way." He pointed, then gave me another charming grin. "I share a house with three other actors. It's not much, but it's home." He looked down at the empty seat across from me. "Would you mind if I joined you?"

I knew it was probably a bad idea, but I wanted some conversation and I didn't know anyone else here. I could keep it platonic and almost business-like. Lawyers went to dinner and out for drinks with clients all the time. It was fine. As long as it didn't cross the line.

The waiter who'd taken my order was coming with my main food, so Taylor and I waited to start a conversation until Taylor's order had been taken. He motioned for me to go ahead with my meal, for which I was grateful. The soup had been amazing, but it hadn't been even close to filling.

"How did your interview go?" Taylor asked as I took a bite of my sandwich.

Wow. This was good. I took a moment to savor the bite before answering Taylor's question with a see-sawing motion of my hand. After I swallowed, I told him a very brief part of the story, mostly how well things had gone with Mr. Duncan but I also mentioned showing up in my room to find DeVon Ricci on the couch. I didn't mention that he was with two naked women or what he had been doing to them, rather choosing to keep it professional and simply say that I'd kicked him out.

Taylor laughed at that, his eyes lighting up. Damn, he was hot. "I did warn you about DeVon."

I nodded and chuckled. "You did."

The waiter returned with Taylor's lunch, some sort of steak sandwich that looked just as good as my turkey one. If I did move out to California, I had a feeling I'd be back here.

"I can't believe you kicked him out of your room," Taylor said before taking a bite of his food.

I shrugged. "It was my room and he was being quite rude."

"Would you kick me out?" Taylor teased.

I chewed slowly on the mouthful I'd just taken. If we were back home or I was just visiting, I knew what the answer would be. Hell, no, I'd ride you like a pony. Unfortunately, that's the kind of answer I most definitely could not give here.

I tried for something safe. "I'd call security on anyone who showed up in my room unannounced and uninvited." I kept my tone flat so it wouldn't sound like I was flirting. I didn't want Taylor to be mad, but I also didn't want him to get the wrong idea. I changed the subject, asking him questions that would be appropriate for a lawyer-client relationship. Details about his work. Where he hoped to be in five years. The kinds of things I could ask anyone without getting too personal.

The problem was, Taylor kept trying to make the answers personal. When I asked about what he saw in his future, I didn't specify his career and he took that latitude to joke about being with a beautiful lawyer. It wasn't that I didn't appreciate what he was saying, but it wasn't making things any easier for me to keep professional.

"Did you rent a car?" he asked as he handed the waiter a credit card with the bill.

I shook my head as I did the same with my bill. I was glad Taylor hadn't tried for an awkward 'I'll pay that.' "The hotel has a car service." I took out my phone. "All I need to do is give them a call."

"Why don't you let me take you back?" Taylor offered.

"I couldn't," I protested.

"Nonsense," he said. "Why have to wait around here for the driver to come get you when I have a car right over there?"

It made sense, I had to admit. I nodded and, after the waiter returned with our receipts and cards, I followed Taylor to a mid-sized Audi. It was nice, but older, definitely more of an up-and-comer type car rather than something an established actor or a mega-star would have. The inside smelled like fast-food and the pine-scented air freshener that hung from the rearview mirror. I couldn't help but smile. Every college guy I'd dated had a car that smelled the same. It was typical bachelor with a menial type job. I suddenly realized that I didn't know what Taylor actually did for a living. If he was only doing local commercials, he had to have either a trust fund or a 'day-job.' I was betting not many kids from Wisconsin had trust funds.

Before I could ask, he looked over at me and asked his own question. "Do you have anything planned the rest of the day?"

I shook my head.

"I was wondering if you'd like to see the ocean. The sun will set in a couple of hours and it's absolutely beautiful over the water. It's not something you'll want to miss."

I hesitated. I really did want to see the ocean and a sunset over the Pacific sounded amazing, but I wasn't sure it was a good idea to be in a car, alone, with Taylor that long. At least eating, we were in public. I didn't want to give anyone the wrong impression.

"It's a half-hour drive," Taylor said, as if he could read my mind. "We'd have some time to enjoy the view, then I could get you back to the hotel before it was even really dark. Plenty of time to rest for your second interview."

After another moment, I nodded. "Let's go."

SEVEN

KRISSY

The Santa Monica Pier. I'd seen it in movies, but it was even more beautiful in real life. The Ferris wheel against the backdrop of blue sky. The sounds and smells that could only be found in a place like this. All of it was everything I'd ever dreamed.

We walked slowly, sometimes talking, sometimes just enjoying the setting sun. Just before the sun reached the horizon, the lights came on, turning the pier into something almost magical. We stopped at a distance so that I could get the entire panoramic view.

I sighed as I leaned against the railing. The smell of salt water mingled with the other scents and I could hear the gentle lapping of water beneath my feet. It was the week after Labor Day, so most of the vacationers had gone home, leaving the pier virtually empty, at least by New York standards. If you weren't pressed shoulder to shoulder with complete strangers, it was almost empty.

I was watching the sun slowly starting to disappear when it happened. Taylor put his hand over mine. I jerked back automatically, turning towards him.

"What do you think you're doing?"

He shrugged, giving me a grin that I was fairly certain he was used to charming the pants off of women. If I hadn't wanted this job so badly, it might've worked for me, too.

"Maybe I'm off here, but I could've sworn I was sensing some attraction."

Dammit. I hadn't been as careful as I'd thought.

"I was under the impression that you liked me."

I sighed again, this time not out of contentment. "I do like you," I confessed. "But you're a client of Mirage. I can't date a potential client." I laughed. "Look, if this was New York and I'd met you there with no strings attached, or even here under different circumstances, I totally would've jumped your bones. But I'm trying to make something of this opportunity." I gave him an apologetic smile. "Sorry."

He took a step towards me, closing the distance down to just a foot between us. "Come on, Krissy." His gaze was heated as it ran down my body and back up again. "I'm just one small client with Mirage, not even close to their top one hundred. They don't give a shit about whether or not we hook up." He reached out and ran the tip of his finger down my arm. "I swear, I won't say a word. No one will ever know."

"I'm sorry, Taylor." I kept my voice cool and firm. "It's not going to happen." I turned my back on him to watch the rest of the sunset. I really hoped he'd take the hint because I wanted to enjoy my view for a bit longer.

He was silent as he moved to stand next to me, but I didn't sense any animosity, which was good. He kept a respectful distance as we finished watching the sunset and I was able to relax and let myself absorb the beauty of what I was seeing. We stayed standing there for several minutes after the last sliver of sun had disappeared, waiting for the first of the stars to begin to come out. The lights from the Pier kept them from being as bright as I knew they'd be out in the country, but it was still far more than I'd ever seen in New York or Chicago.

Finally, I pushed back from the rail and broke the silence. "I should be getting back."

He nodded and flashed me a polite smile that made me feel like perhaps things would be okay between us. That was good. As bad as it would be to date a client, I had a feeling Mirage wouldn't look too fondly on a client being pissed at me either.

We made small talk on the ride back to my hotel, keeping it light and nothing personal. By the time he pulled up in front of the hotel, I had regained the sense of wonder I'd had when I'd first stepped off the plane.

"So," he said as he flashed that beautiful white smile again, "What do you say to a night-cap in the bar?" He winked at me. "Or in your suite?"

He was like a dog with a bone.

"You're super cute and very persistent." I kept my voice polite. "But I can't do this. You're a client and I'm taking this job possibility very seriously."

If anything, his grin widened. "But what if you don't get the job?"

Now I was annoyed. Persistence was one thing, but if he kept pushing it, even his pretty face and rock-hard body weren't going to be enough to keep me from saying something I'd regret. "If I don't get it, and you're ever in New York, look me up." I opened the door. "I'm sure you'd be fun for a couple days." I didn't wait to hear a response, but rather climbed out of the car and headed for the front doors.

I really hoped that put an end to it. I so didn't need a client stalker.

EIGHT

KRISSY

This time when I was called out of the reception area, I was taken to the elevator I'd seen yesterday. The receptionist didn't say a word as we reached the second floor and the doors opened. She just gestured for me to go ahead without her. Based on what I'd seen yesterday with Mr. Ricci, I had a feeling he was the type of man who appreciated a strong woman. At least professionally. Something about him told me that in his personal life, it might be a bit different.

I stepped off the elevator and knocked on the heavy wooden door now directly in front of me.

"Come in." An annoyingly familiar voice came from the other side of the door.

As I stepped inside, I saw that DeVon's office didn't look like the rest of the building. Instead of glass and metal, his office was dark with a heavy curtain covering what must have been a window at his back. He had heavy wooden furniture that matched the door I'd knocked on. The color scheme was dark brown and a deep red that almost looked like blood. It looked like something out of a *Godfather* movie. Or a vampire flick.

DeVon was sitting behind his desk and didn't get up when I closed the door behind me. I really hoped that wasn't his normal way of behaving and he wasn't only being an ass to me because of yesterday. I walked towards him, waiting for him to look up from the paper he was reading and greet me. He didn't. In fact, all he did was point to one of the chairs in front of the desk.

I was tempted to take the other one, just to see what he'd do, but I didn't. As much as he annoyed me, being intentionally antagonistic wasn't a good idea. No matter how much I wanted to.

I crossed one leg over the other, folded my hands in my lap and waited. I was normally impatient and impulsive, at least according to my friends, but when it came to a battle of the wills and sheer stubbornness, winning trumped everything else.

Finally, after what was probably a good ten minutes, he closed the paper and set it aside. His expression was unreadable as he looked at me. "Krissy Jensen, I liked how you handled the situation yesterday."

Apparently, he didn't believe in opening with small talk. That was fine with me. The less time I had to spend with him, the better. He might have been pretty to look at, but I wasn't fond of the attitude.

"That was a test, you know."

No shit. I didn't say that, of course. "I figured that much. A little unusual, I must say." Carrie would've been proud of my self-control.

"What can I say?" He shrugged. "I do things differently." His eyes narrowed, studying me. "I don't like fake people, and this town has too many of them already. I want one hundred percent honesty and trust from all my employees. In return, I don't bullshit them, either." He rested his hands on his desk. "Do you think you can do that? Be honest no matter what?"

That was an easy one for me to answer. "Absolutely. And I couldn't agree more. I hate liars."

He was silent for several minutes and I could feel his eyes boring into me, like he was trying to read something deep inside and determine if I was telling the truth. I tried very hard not to fidget. I'd never been very good at sitting still, and his heavy gaze wasn't making it any easier.

Finally, he spoke. "I'm not so sure you can be completely honest." He leaned back in his chair and set his elbows on the armrests. He pressed his fingertips together and peered at me over them. "How do I know you're not just saying that to get the job?"

I tried not to take offense at the question. He had a right to be suspicious. Some people would've had a problem promising honesty and actually delivering. For me, I actually liked that he required it. In fact, his statement about liars was probably the first thing I actually liked about him.

"I would say to trust me, but if you don't believe I'm telling the truth, it doesn't matter what I say."

He inclined his head, leading me to believe he approved of my answer. "I could conduct the interview in an...unusual way to determine if you will provide me with answers you believe I will want to hear or if you will answer honestly, no matter what you think my opinion will be."

That sounded like a very bad idea.

"I have found," he continued, "that if I ask questions of a personal nature – a very personal nature – I can determine if they are lying or not."

Yeah, agreeing to this 'unusual' interview was definitely not a good idea.

"A benefit of this will be that I will be able to provide you with a yes or no regarding the job once we are finished."

He was tempting my impatience, but that wasn't the main reason I wanted to agree. He'd caught me off guard yesterday, and while I'd managed to recover nicely, he'd still shocked me. I had a feeling whatever he was going to ask would be sexually loaded and he wanted to see if I'd crack. It wasn't just about honesty. It was about seeing if I could handle the pressure of working in a place like this. Whether I got the job or not, I was determined to let him know that he couldn't break me.

"All right," I agreed.

I could see a pleased light in his eyes for a brief second before it was gone again.

"My questions will deal with things that you may not feel are appropriate for a work situation, and I will not take kindly should you decide to complain after having agreed to this interview." His tone was sharp as he gave me the warning.

"I'm waiting for the first question," I said mildly. No way was I backing down.

He chuckled. "Then we begin." He crossed one long leg over the other. "Are you a virgin?"

I almost rolled my eyes, but remembered that I needed to keep it professional, no matter how unprofessional the questions were. "No."

"What were the circumstances surrounding your first sexual encounter?"

One side of my mouth quirked up. "I was fifteen, and my boyfriend and I did it in the back of his car." I raised an eyebrow as if to ask him if that was all he had.

"And your most recent sexual encounter?" He didn't react to either my answer or my change in facial expression.

"I hooked up with a guy at my friend's burlesque club. I think his name was Frank." If that didn't tell him I had no problem being honest, I didn't know what would.

"Do you make a habit of fucking strangers?"

Okay, so that's how we were going to play it.

"I do it sometimes, but I wouldn't consider it a habit," I admitted. I'd never been ashamed of my sex life and I wasn't about to begin now.

"But you refused to join me yesterday."

"That's not a question," I retorted.

This time, his lips definitely twitched. "You're right. My question then: what was the reason for declining my invitation?"

I almost cringed. He wanted me to be honest, but I knew he wasn't going to like my answer. "Two reasons. One, I don't fuck my boss, or potential boss. Two, you were being an asshole."

He did smile this time, and it was all I could do not to smile in response.

"Have you ever slept with someone you worked with?"

I nodded. "Co-workers, yes, but never someone in a position above or below me." I bit back a laugh at the obvious joke there.

"Have you ever had sex with someone in exchange for a favor?"

I frowned. "Does sleeping with my college tutor count?" When DeVon didn't answer, I clarified, "That wasn't how I paid him. It was more like a bonus...for both of us. But, no, I don't ask for things in return for sex."

He nodded, but I couldn't tell what he thought about my answer. "Have you ever dated a client?"

I noticed the change in verb but didn't ask about it. "It depends on your definition of client."

"Spoken like a true lawyer," he said.

"I haven't slept with or dated anyone who was my direct client," I answered. "But I have had relationships with men who were clients of other lawyers in the firm where I worked."

"You understand that this is not acceptable at Mirage," he said, his tone almost scolding.

My temper flared. How dare he talk to me like he was on some high moral ground? I didn't snap at him, though. Instead, I said, "Completely. I would never consider propositioning anyone involved with the company, or accepting a proposition from someone Mirage represents. It would be unprofessional."

A flash of amusement crossed his features, and I knew he'd

understood my dig at his behavior yesterday. "Do you consider yourself sexually adventurous?"

I couldn't quite stop myself from being a bit saucy in return. "I'm always open to new experiences."

"Good to know."

I shifted in my seat as I felt a sudden zing of arousal. Dammit. I didn't care how sexy his voice sounded when he'd said that. He was going to be my boss. And he was an asshole. Both reasons why I hadn't slept with him yesterday were still applicable today.

"Do you have any problems taking orders?"

That question made me blink because I wasn't entirely sure if he was still asking sexual questions or if he'd switched to more job relevant inquiries since he was satisfied I was telling the truth. Something in his dark eyes told me that his question wasn't entirely innocent.

Two could play at that game.

"It depends on who gives them," I answered coolly. "I'm no pushover, but I also don't have a problem obeying someone in charge. If he's...worthy."

This time, DeVon was the one shifting in his chair. He made it look like he was just switching legs, but I had a feeling it was actually something else. The air had a thickness to it that hadn't been there a moment ago.

"Are you willing to accept...consequences for wrong behavior?"

"As long as the required behavior, and all possible consequences, are spelled out beforehand." I was now very sure that he was lacing his questions with double meaning and I fed my answers out the same way. "I don't think it's right to expect behavior that isn't explained."

He nodded, and I could see that he agreed. He leaned forward and rested his hands on his desk again. "It seems to me that you were indeed telling the truth. I have to consult with Mr. Duncan, but we will have answer for you tomorrow before you fly home."

Once again, my mouth decided to act before my brain could intervene. "Who's being dishonest now? You told me if I went along with your interview, you'd tell me yes or no at the end of it."

He smiled, and I wondered if that had been another test, one to see if I was willing to hold others to the same standard to which I was being held. "I did promise that," he said. "Perhaps I was too hasty. What I can tell you is that your answers mean you're still in the running. Had I not been pleased with what you said, I would've just told you no and sent you home."

He picked up his paper again and I knew the interview was over. I stood. I would just have to be satisfied with what he gave me. My stomach gave a little twist as my brain automatically translated my innocent statement into an innuendo. Shit. His questioning had got me thinking that way and now it was going to take forever to stop.

I really disliked that man.

NINE

KRISSY

I was considering heading back down to Sunset Plaza for lunch again but as soon as I stepped into the hotel lobby, I knew I was going to have to go somewhere else, just to avoid the awkward moment I was currently experiencing as Taylor beamed at me from where he was leaning against the front desk.

"Krissy." He took a step forward. "I just got an invite to this fancy party in the Hills tonight and was wondering if you wanted to come with me."

I was shaking my head before he'd even finished speaking. "No."

He held up his hands in a gesture of surrender. "It's not a date. I was just thinking that you might want to come because there are going to be a lot of actors and potential clients. It'll be a great chance to mingle." He added, "Think of how good it'll look when you get the job if you already know the names of clients as they come in."

He had a point. I crossed my arms and gave him a stern look.

"All right," I said. "I'll go." He opened his mouth to speak and I held up a finger. "Only if you stop flirting."

He grinned. "I can't promise anything one hundred percent, especially if I get some alcohol in my system, but I'll do my best."

A try was probably the best I could hope for. I nodded. "Okay."

"Great!" He turned and did that thing where he was walking backwards and talking to me at the same time. I'd seen it on movies but didn't think anyone actually did it. "I'll pick you up a little before eight. We want to make an entrance, after all."

I couldn't believe I was going to my first Hollywood party! I smiled so widely that it hurt my mouth. This was going to be amazing! I took two steps towards the elevator and realized that I didn't have anything to wear. I'd brought a business outfit for a second interview, comfortable clothes for the flight home tomorrow and two cute dresses for sight-seeing. None of those were going to be right for a party in the Hills. I should've brought my green dress, the one Carrie referred to as Christmas ribbon.

I looked at the concierge. "Is the car available?"

He nodded. "Any specific destination in mind, Miss Jensen?"

I smiled again. I was going to fulfill another of my fantasies. A Beverly Hills shopping trip.

When I told the driver where I wanted to go, my day got even better. His sister worked at Barneys. That was exactly what I needed. Someone in the know of what was hot in Hollywood right now. On the ride over, the driver told me all about Jamie and how she was working towards becoming a fashion designer. Like I'd said before. Hollywood was where everyone wanted to be something else.

The moment I stepped into the store, I felt like I was in heaven. I'd gone to one of the most elite boutiques in New York with Carrie, but that had been different. Even though Gavin had bought me something, we'd been shopping for her. Today was all about me.

"Miss Jensen?" A cute little thing with strawberry blond curls came bounding up to me. I could tell she was one of those people who always had too much energy and never walked anywhere. She also looked like she was twelve, even though I'd been told she was nineteen.

"Jamie." I smiled at her.

"My brother said you were going to a party in the Hills?"

I nodded.

"I have just the thing." She motioned for me to follow her. "We just got this in today. In fact, we're not even technically done putting them on the floor yet."

I was starting to have my doubts about the young woman's ability to pick a dress as we passed gorgeous dress after gorgeous dress. Then she stopped in front of the most beautiful dress I'd ever seen.

"I had a couple in mind since I didn't know what your coloring was, but as soon as I saw you, I knew this would be perfect."

I had to agree. If it looked as good on me as I thought it was going to, Jamie had just outdone herself. She handed it to me and pointed me to the dressing rooms. I maneuvered into the slinky garment and zipped up the side. It fit like a glove.

I turned so I could see my reflection. The hem hit me at a little above mid-thigh, high enough that I knew I was going to have to be careful how I moved or I'd flash someone. The neckline plunged down between my breasts, revealing quite a bit of flesh without being tacky. The color was a rich purple that brought out the blue-black highlights in my hair. I'd never been so in love with a dress in my life.

I stepped out and Jamie voiced her approval. Then I saw the price tag and my stomach sank. Four hundred dollars. I couldn't afford that.

"I'll give you my discount," Jamie said, correctly interpreting my expression. "It's thirty percent off."

I made a face. That was still a lot of money.

"You look amazing in that dress," Jamie said. "I can show you other ones that will look good on you, but nothing like that one."

She was right. I looked at the number again. I had spent more than that on shoes before. I made up my mind. "I'll take it."

Jamie let out a squeal of delight, and I couldn't help but laugh. She was adorable.

We chatted as she rang me up and continued to talk on my way out to the car. She talked to him then for several minutes before he was able to remind her that they were both still working. She took his gentle reminder in good stride and waved at us as we drove away.

"Back to the hotel," I said. I would order room service so I could take my time getting ready. I was going to make sure that I was nothing short of breath-taking tonight. It would be my first impression on some of Hollywood and I wanted it to be a good one.

TEN

KRISSY

I had to admit that I was a little nervous. New York was big and busy, full of interesting and exciting people, but LA was different. I knew I was hot. I'd had men and women telling me that since I hit puberty, but this was the place where all of the beautiful people gathered. But, when I saw the expression on Taylor's face when I met him outside the hotel, my confidence was bolstered. Jamie had definitely picked the right dress.

Now I just had to focus on not looking like the wide-eyed newcomer, completely mesmerized by the glam and glitter. When we pulled up in front of a pair of massive iron gates, it was more difficult than I'd expected not to gawk. I'd grown up with money, but there was a huge difference between the elegant old money of Chicago high society and Hollywood money. I mean, my family had a couple maids and groundskeepers, and we had a driver because my mom hated driving herself, but the way high society showed their wealth was in art and with charity. This was definitely flashier. First of all, there was a valet waiting.

Taylor grinned. "It's typical for parties in the Hills to have valet service, especially the ones on these windy, narrow roads."

I nodded. That actually made sense. It didn't make it less impressive, but at least I knew it wasn't just some sort of pretentious thing. Taylor and I walked up to the large, muscular man who stood in front of the gates. Bar or mansion, there was no mistaking a bouncer. Taylor gave the man his name and introduced me as his plus one. I bristled, but didn't contradict him. Now that I was here, I wanted to go inside.

The bouncer nodded and the lock on the gates clicked. He pushed them open and we started up the driveway. It wasn't a long one, but it had a curve that kept the house from sight until we went around it. As soon as I saw it, I corrected my mental labeling of the place as a house. This was a mansion.

In New York, the rich lived in expensive lofts and had homes in the Hamptons. In Chicago, it was very similar. My family owned a house in the city and three vacation homes that included a cottage in Maine, a beach house in North Carolina and a villa in Italy. Our main house was one of the bigger ones in our affluent neighborhood, but it couldn't truly be called a mansion. In fact, it was half the size of this one. All columns and arches, some impressive architecture that I had no name for, and landscaping that had to cost more than my entire firm made in a year. As Taylor and I stepped inside the mansion, we were treated to a breathtaking view of the city lights through a panoramic glass wall, and waiters carrying finger food weaving between all of the beautiful people.

I was so busy staring at everything that I didn't see the waitress heading my way until her arm hit mine. I side-stepped, narrowly avoiding getting something that looked like caviar all over my dress. The tray crashed to the ground, spraying food across the floor.

"I am so sorry!" The waitress was a cute little blonde who looked a little younger than me. Her face was red, and her eyes were wide, one of those 'deer-in-headlights' expressions on her face. "Damnit! So stupid!"

"It's okay," I tried saying.

"No, no it's not." She was shaking her head and I could see tears forming in her dark eyes. She looked up at me. "Please don't tell my boss. I'm so sorry. Please don't tell him. He'll fire me."

"Hey, it's okay." I put my hand on her shoulder, hoping the contact would break through. "No harm done."

A look of relief washed over her face and I started to smile.

"Elise!"

Her face fell, and I turned towards the voice. A man was striding towards us, his face red with anger. He got in the girl's face, his eyes narrowed.

"Go get your things, you're done!" He didn't even bother trying to keep his voice down.

"It was my fault." The words popped out of my mouth and I went with it. "I wasn't watching where I was going and I bumped into her." I gave the man what I hoped was a sheepish-looking smile. "Sorry."

The man looked at me for a moment, as if trying to decide if he wanted to believe me, then he shook his head and turned back to Elise. He scowled at her, but his voice was back at a normal level when he spoke again. "Clean up the mess and get back to work. There are plenty more trays to be handed out."

Elise waited until the man was out of earshot, then said, "Thank you for covering for me."

I shrugged. "Anytime." I shot a glance at the man's back as he disappeared back through the door he'd come through. "What an asshole."

Elise gave me a brief smile. "Good luck."

Before I could ask what she meant, she hurried away, presumably to find something to clean up with. Did she think the guy was going to come back and call me a liar?

I didn't have time to think about it anymore, though, because the music had changed and Taylor grabbed my hand and pulled me towards the dance floor. If there was one place I felt comfortable around a bunch of gorgeous strangers, it was on the dance floor. Some of the women here might've been prettier than me, but I knew I could dance, and not just well, but good enough to have all of the straight men and more than a few women thinking about what it would be like to get me in bed.

For an hour, I forgot about everything else but the club music pounding around me. I danced with Taylor, but let myself move around as well, turning around to move with one stranger, then another. Never touching, always just out of reach. The air was electric and I'd never felt so alive.

"I need some air," Taylor practically shouted in my ear.

I nodded and let him lead me outside. For people who lived in rural areas, the one-acre backyard might not have seemed that big, but for someone who'd lived in Chicago and then New York, it was huge, and absolutely gorgeous.

Taylor started down the stairs and I fell in step next to him. We walked along a stone path that curved through the grass, heading for the fence at the far end.

"What do you think?" he asked.

"It's beautiful," I answered, craning my neck to see the stars. It was too bright to see them all, but I could still see them better than I could back home.

"You're beautiful."

I looked over at him, opening my mouth to tell him that he couldn't say things like that.

"I can't explain it," he said before I could speak. "I'm drawn to you."

He reached out and grabbed my hand, his fingers warm as they curled around mine. I knew I should pull away, but I was frozen to the spot. Then he was leaning towards me and, for a brief moment, I was tempted. He was so hot and his lips looked so soft. I wanted to know if he was as good a kisser as I thought he would be. What harm would there be in one kiss?

I sighed and took a step back, taking my hand from his. "You promised," I said. I had to look away so he couldn't see how close I'd been to letting him kiss me.

"Come on, Krissy," he coaxed. "Why are you doing this? I know you want it, too."

Apparently, I hadn't looked away fast enough. I turned back towards him. "Maybe I do," I admitted. "But I can't. You're Mirage's client and there's a strict policy about not dating clients. You know that."

I didn't add that if I didn't get the job, I just might call him up and take him for a ride or two. At least then I'd get something good out of this trip. I looked over towards the pool just as a couple guests stripped off their tops and jumped in.

"I should get back," I said. "I have a final interview tomorrow and I don't want to screw anything up."

Taylor sighed and I could hear the disappointment. "Come on, I'll take you back."

The ride back to my hotel was quiet and a little awkward, but at least Taylor didn't try anything. If I got the job, I'd be able to get past the flirtations and the almost-kiss, but if he tried again, we might have a problem if I had to work with him in the future.

He pulled up in front of the hotel and put the car in park so he could turn to face me. I really hoped he wasn't going to make a pass after having come all this way without one. I wasn't sure how many rejections he could take before he'd get mad.

"I hope you get the job," he said sincerely.

"Thank you," I replied, startled. That had been nice of him. I got out of the car.

As I moved to shut the door, he spoke again, "I'd like it if you stuck around."

He waited until I reached the hotel doors before he drove away. Maybe he was more than a gentleman than I'd given him credit for. I smiled as I rode the elevator up to my room. After my encounter with Mr. Ricci, I hadn't been sure those existed anymore.

ELEVEN

KRISSY

You'd think that the third time I found myself sitting in the lobby of Mirage Talent, I'd be less nervous, but that wasn't the case. My plane was leaving in an hour and I'd gotten a call from one of the receptionists saying that I needed to come in for a third interview, at which time a decision would be made. I wasn't just nervous, though; I was pissed. After all the shit DeVon Ricci had pulled and all his talk about honesty, he was jerking me around, asking me to come in again rather than just telling me what he and Mr. Duncan had decided.

"Mr. Ricci will see you now." The receptionist's tone told me that she'd had to repeat herself. She waited for me to stand and then followed me to the elevator. "He said to go ahead in without knocking." She gave me a polite smile. "Good luck."

I scrubbed my palms against my hips as I waited for the elevator to reach the next floor. I didn't like the idea of walking into Mr. Ricci's office without knocking, especially not after what I'd found in my hotel room. For all I knew, he'd be in there with one or both of those women again, maybe doing more than he'd been doing before. Snapshots flipped through my brain of DeVon fucking those two women in a variety of positions. Then they disappeared and it was just him, waiting for me.

"Damnit," I swore softly. I didn't want to think about Mr. Ricci that way, even if I didn't get the job. My friends often told me that I had shit taste in men, but even I wasn't dumb enough to fall for someone like that.

When the doors opened, I lifted my chin and walked out, exuding my usual confidence. If I couldn't get rid of the nerves, I could at least pretend I didn't feel them. I didn't even hesitate as I opened the door. Hesitation would've made me think twice, and I didn't want that. I had to pretend I was even more confident than I felt.

The room was fairly dark, thanks to the curtains being drawn, but this time, the chair behind the desk was empty. The whole room was empty. I didn't let it stop me. I walked over to the chair where I'd sat before and took a seat, crossing my ankles and waiting.

After a few seconds, I heard a toilet flush and a door to my right opened. Mr. Ricci appeared, his face impossible to read.

"Ms. Jensen, so glad you could come again."

Like I'd really had a choice if I wanted the job.

"I would tell you to sit down, but I can see you already helped yourself."

It was on the tip of my tongue to retort that if he'd really been that concerned about me sitting on my own, he should've been here when I came in, or waited until he really was ready for me to have the receptionist send me up. I didn't say either of those things, however. I wasn't going to give him the satisfaction of knowing he'd pushed my buttons.

We sat in silence for a few minutes and I wondered if he was waiting for me to break. I thought I'd proven before that I was patient.

"Congratulations," he said suddenly. "You're hired."

I stared at him for a second, confused. "Excuse me? I'm hired? What about that third interview your receptionist mentioned?"

He met my eyes and I felt a little thrill go through me. "That was last night." His lips curved into an enigmatic little smile.

Now I was really confused.

"At my house," he explained without waiting for me to ask. "You passed all the tests." He pressed his fingertips together in front of him. "I liked how you called that prick of a waiter an asshole. After all, he almost fired that poor actress wanna-be simply because she spilled some food." He chuckled, as if the entire thing amused him.

"Your house?" I said, my voice sounding faint in my ears. He'd played me? "That whole thing was a set-up? You were behind it all? Made her bump into me?"

He raised an eyebrow. "I had to see what you would do in a situation like that." He added, "You did well."

I scowled. He'd embarrassed me, almost ruined my new dress, and all for what? What kind of interview was that? I was just applying for an associate position in the legal department, not trying to become CEO. Suddenly, what he'd said clicked. I tried not to sound as pissed as I was, and it wasn't easy. "You said I passed ALL the tests. What else was there?"

He looked pleased that I'd asked. "Taylor, of course. He's another wanna-be actor I hired to try to seduce you."

My stomach dropped even as my temper flared. He'd hired Taylor to try to seduce me? How fucking humiliating! If a guy wasn't attracted to me, that was fine, but to have someone be hired to pretend to be into me...It was one thing too many.

I stood and turned towards the door, fully intending to storm out and slam the door behind me for good measure. I was almost close enough to reach the doorknob when he stepped between me and the door. I had too much momentum and ended up only a few inches away from DeVon when I stopped.

"If you leave this office, you go home," he warned. I could feel the tension between us thicken, making it hard to breathe.

"Fine," I snapped. I tried to reach around him, but he was blocking the doorknob.

"Let me explain."

I looked up at him, only now realizing just how big he was. He had to be at least six three, if not taller, and I knew that under his expensive and well-tailored suit was a lean, but defined chest. He was way too close, but I wasn't going to back down. "There's nothing to explain. You're a narcissistic prick." And there went the job offer, but I didn't care. I'd only said the truth.

His eyes hardened, turning cold. "We all look after ourselves first. Even you."

My fingers curled into fists as I resisted the urge to slap him. How dare he tell me what I would and wouldn't do! "Not if it means hurting someone else."

He laughed and the sound was bitter. "You can stop pretending. You already got the job."

"I said I'd be honest, remember?" I snapped back. "And you can shove your job. I can find an associate's position somewhere else."

One side of his mouth tipped up in a smile. "I'm not offering some little position in the legal department. Do you really think I'd go through all of this if you were just going to work for Duncan?"

I took a step back. Being too close to him was messing with me. I had no idea what he was talking about.

"You'll be working for me."

I laughed, shaking my head. "As your assistant? No thanks." I stepped to the side and reached for the doorknob again. He'd moved just enough so that I could reach it.

He grabbed my arm and it was like a jolt of electricity went through me. I'd never had my body react to a simple touch that way and I told myself it was just because tensions were running high.

"You wouldn't be my assistant, Krissy."

I swallowed hard as he said my first name. I liked the way it sounded more than I wanted to.

He continued, "You'd be an associate, but one who was being groomed to become a partner in a few years. Your starting salary would be a hundred and twenty thousand dollars a year."

He let go of my arm but I didn't move. I was too shocked to do anything but stand there. He walked back to his desk, nothing in his demeanor to hint at what had just happened.

"Be here tomorrow at nine a.m. We'll discuss closing your affairs in New York then."

I opened the door and walked to the elevator without a word. What the hell had just happened?

TWELVE

DEVON

I paced from one end of the room to the other, my entire body tense. I'd come back from my late lunch to find that I'd missed three calls from a director saying that one of Mirage's clients had shown up to set late, drunk or high. Now the movie was behind schedule and the director was pissed. The fact that it had gotten all the way to me meant that one of my people wasn't doing his or her job right. Rather than call the director and try to smooth things over – which wasn't my fucking job – I was currently tearing the actor's manager a new one.

"I don't care if you have to clean up his vomit, shower and dress him to get him to the set ready to go. You fix this, or you won't only be fired, you'll find yourself blackballed from every agency in town. You won't be able to book a porn star for *Blow-job Betty 6*, you understand me?"

I saw the door open and turned towards it. Duncan came in, giving me an impatient gesture that said he wanted to talk.

"Can you wait a fucking second?" I snapped at him.

"What?" The manager on the other end of my Bluetooth now sounded confused as well as scared.

"Not you," I said. "You do whatever you need to do to make sure your client does his fucking job or we're through with him, too. Pretty-boy actors are a dime a dozen in this city. You tell him that if he fucks up again, he'll be bottoming in gay porn again to pay his rent."

I hung up before my almost-ex-employee could say anything, and then turned towards Duncan. He didn't even wait for me to ask him what he wanted, which pissed me off almost as much as what he had to say.

"I hear you offered the job to Ms. Jensen. You didn't think it would be a good idea to discuss it with me first, since she'll be working for me?" His tone was terse.

"Calm down," I said as I sat down in my chair. I motioned to one of the chairs, but Duncan stayed standing. "I didn't hire Ms. Jensen for your position. You can have your boring little what's-her-name. I have other plans for Ms. Jensen."

Duncan's eyes narrowed. "Like what? Your mistress?"

I laughed. "Do you honestly think I need to pay women to have sex with me?" I shook my head. "Besides, I don't shit where I eat." My smiled faded. "Now get the fuck out of my office."

I leaned forward and pressed my intercom. "Monica, get Clark Morris from ACU Pictures on the phone." I had damage control. I glanced up and saw that Duncan was still standing there, staring at me, his mouth hanging open as if what I'd said had shocked him. "You're still here? Don't you have work to do?"

Duncan's jaw snapped shut and he turned and hurried away.

I leaned back in my chair, waiting for Morris. I wasn't thinking about Clark Morris, though. I was thinking about my newest hire. Krissy Jensen. I liked the way her name felt in my mouth, like it was meant for me to say.

She hadn't said yes to the offer, and she had walked off without acknowledging my instructions to come in tomorrow, but I knew she'd accept. No one in their right mind would turn down an opportunity like this. And no one said no to me.

A part of me wondered if Krissy would be the exception to that rule. The idea of this beautiful woman being strong enough to go toe-to-toe with me turned me on. She was the kind of woman a man like me dreamed about. My cock hardened at the thought of doing exactly what I'd said I wouldn't do and taking my relationship with Krissy far beyond employer / employee.

Fuck. Just the thought of her on her knees, her calling me Sir and Master, taking her against a wall hard and fast...

I grabbed my cell phone and scrolled through my contacts until I found the one I wanted.

"Hello?" The woman's voice was sultry even with that single word.

I didn't bother with any pleasantries or greetings. "Meet me at our usual place in an hour. I need a release."

THIRTEEN

KRISSY

He made me miss my fucking plane. I'd been so rattled when I'd arrived at the airport with barely enough time to get through security that I'd gone to the wrong gate. And even better than that, there wasn't another normal flight out until tomorrow afternoon. I was supposed to be back in the office tomorrow, ready to tell Mimi if I was putting in my two-week notice or not. I had two options. I could take the redeye that left later that evening or call Mimi and tell her that I'd missed my flight and take an extra day's vacation, which would mean going back to the hotel to see if I could have my room back, or trying to find another one on my own dime. After what I'd said to Mr. Ricci, there was no way he could be serious about me still having the job.

And losing it didn't bother me at all. I didn't want to work with someone who'd told me he valued honesty, then lied about everything. He'd played me, and manipulated the situation, trying to provoke whatever response it was his twisted little mind wanted. I still couldn't believe he'd hired Taylor to try to seduce me. I had to give Taylor credit for being convincing, I thought bitterly. I'd really thought he wanted me, and finding out that it had all been a lie hurt.

I couldn't work with a person who cared that little about other people's feelings. Most people thought divorce lawyers were vicious, sharks who attacked when they smelled blood in the water. DeVon made us seem like cuddly puppies.

I bought my redeye ticket and went to the bar to wait. I had some time to kill, but I didn't want to risk being late again. Having a couple drinks while I called Carrie to ask her to pick me up sounded like a good idea.

"I thought you'd be in the air now," Carrie said as soon as she answered.

She sounded out of breath and I wondered if she was busy moving boxes in her new office or if she and Gavin were enjoying their more flexible schedule to have a bit of afternoon fun.

"I missed my flight," I said. "But I'm catching the redeye home."

"What's wrong?" Her tone changed immediately. "You sound upset."

"Pissed about my flight," I said.

"You didn't get the job." Carrie wasn't fooled by my explanation.

I sighed and took a sip of the drink I'd ordered. I wanted to down it in one go, but I had some time to kill and if I drank like that the whole time, I'd have to be carried onto the plane.

"No, I got it," I said. "But I can't work for someone like that. He's a total perv."

"A perv?"

Now Carrie sounded mad as well as concerned and I mentally scolded myself. I should've known better. She was going to think DeVon was like our former client, Howard Weiss, who'd used and abused women before selling them as sex slaves.

"What happened?"

"It's not what you think," I said. "But he's an ass. I'll tell you the whole story when I see you." And now came the real reason for my call. "Can you pick me up?"

"Sure," Carrie agreed. "What time will you be in?"

"Three in the morning."

"Shit," she grumbled. "Guess it's a good thing I'm my own boss, right? I'll be there."

"Thanks, Carrie," I said.

"No problem. I'll see you then."

We ended the call and I turned to the serious business of drinking and reading a new romance novel I'd downloaded a couple days ago. That, at least, should keep me distracted enough not to get too wasted. I just wanted to take the edge off, not be black-out drunk.

I was pleasantly buzzed by the time I was supposed to board the plane. I could walk without stumbling, speak without slurring my words, but I also wasn't feeling much of the tension from the past few days. Unfortunately, I wasn't relaxed enough to sleep on the plane. Every time I'd close my eyes, I'd get these images. Taylor trying to kiss me. DeVon on the couch in my hotel room, his shirt open enough to expose his six pack. The admiration on Taylor's face when he'd seen me in that dress. The heat in DeVon's eyes when he'd stopped me from leaving his office. None of these made for a pleasant flight.

I was exhausted by the time the plane landed and hoped that Carrie wasn't running late. I just wanted to go home and sleep. As soon as I stepped outside, I saw her car and gave a sigh of relief. I tossed my bag in the back and climbed into the passenger's seat. She leaned over to give me a quick hug before speaking.

"Spill."

I didn't need her to clarify. I knew what she wanted to know. She started to drive and I started to talk. I was tired enough that what little filter I had between my brain and my mouth was gone, so I didn't hold anything back, including every detail of what I'd seen in my hotel room and the whole elaborate interview scheme.

It wasn't until she started laughing that I realized how completely insane it all sounded.

"Wow," she said when I finished. "He's completely crazy."

I had to laugh at that. She was right.

"But," she continued. "That probably makes him normal for Hollywood, right? We've all heard the stories." She grinned at me. "Besides, I thought the crazy was part of the attraction for you."

I glared at her, but wasn't really annoyed. This is why I needed Carrie. She and I helped each other not to take things so seriously all the time. "Funny," I said. "You haven't met the guy, though." I sighed. I had to be honest with her. "It'd be a much easier decision if he wasn't hot as hell. I don't think I can trust myself around him."

Carrie's smile widened. "I can relate to that."

I knew she could. For a while, we'd both thought Gavin was bad news and Carrie had been torn between what she'd wanted and what we thought was good for her.

"About the job, though," she said. "Krissy, you have to follow your gut, but know that an opportunity like this doesn't come around very often. If you give this up because this DeVon guy can be kind of an ass, or because you think he's hot, will you be able to live with that decision?"

I didn't answer. She was right. If the job offer was still on the table, I would've had to consider that, but I doubted Mr. Ricci was going to keep pursuing me. Aside from the number of insults I'd thrown at him, I'd also flown back to New York without giving him an official answer. When I didn't show up later this morning, he'd figure it out.

"Whatever you do, I'll support you," Carrie said as she pulled up in front of my building.

I nodded, thanked her for the ride and then headed upstairs. I didn't even bother to shower or undress. I kicked off my shoes, dropped my bag next to my bed and flopped down on the bedspread. This time, I didn't have any problem falling asleep.

My alarm woke me far too soon and I was in a daze as I showered and dressed. The apartment was quiet without Carrie there. Her things were all packed and ready to go this weekend, but she stayed with Gavin most nights anyway. She'd promised me this weekend, but a part of me wished she would've stayed last night. It would've been nice to at least see her while I downed my first cup of coffee before heading out the door.

The caffeine was starting to kick in by the time I reached the coffee shop where I ordered my usual, but with an extra shot of espresso. I was going to be wired, but the alternative was sleepy and that wouldn't do. I had to prove to Mimi that I wanted to be there, even though I'd rather be on the West Coast, working for Mirage.

Mimi was on the phone when I got there so I just waved, then headed for my desk. My friends, Leslie Calvin and Dena Monroe, smiled at me as I passed and I knew they'd want the scoop on what had happened, but I didn't want to go over it again just yet. I called out that I'd talk to them at lunch and continued to my desk. Since I'd technically been on vacation, there were memos and files waiting for me regarding cases I was assigned to, so I had plenty to keep me busy. I began to go through them, making a list of who I had to call back in order of importance.

I was in the middle of the list when my phone rang.

"Webster and Steinberg, Krissy Jensen speaking."

"I thought we'd had an understanding."

I froze. There was no way in hell that the voice on the other end of my phone was DeVon Ricci. I had to be hallucinating, right?

"You were supposed to be in my office this morning, not back in New York, pissing your life away as a divorce attorney."

"What do you want?" I kept my voice low, not wanting anyone around me to think that I was talking to a client so rudely.

"I believe I made that quite clear," he said. "I want you."

I swallowed hard and shifted in my seat. He shouldn't have been able to make those three words, which were intended professionally, sound so sensual.

"I enjoyed our little games."

My temper flared. "Games? You think it's funny playing with people like that? I'm not about to work for someone who manipulates people like some sort of demented puppet-master. People aren't toys for your amusement, jackass."

He was silent for a minute and I thought that maybe I'd gone far enough that he'd back off. I wasn't sure how I felt about that.

"How about I sweeten the deal?"

My eyebrows shot up. Was he serious? That's how he responded to me being rude?

"You'll have your own office with your own PA. I'll personally oversee your training and slowly assign clients to you as I see you're ready."

"Why me?" I asked the question that had been nagging at the back of my mind since I'd gotten the offer. "Why in the world would you make an offer like this to someone like me? I have no experience, no qualifications."

"You're a Columbia graduate who passed the bar," he said. "I wouldn't sell yourself short."

Now he was just making fun of me. "I don't have any experience in your field. The legal department, sure, but not as an agent."

"You're more than qualified," he said. "Compared to most agents, you're overqualified. Your contract skills will help you when you're negotiating with clients and production companies. Rather than needing a lawyer to look over everything, you'll be able to do it all on your own."

Okay, he had a point there, but if that was the case, why didn't he only hire lawyers?

He answered my question without me having to ask it. "That's one reason, but you have other qualities that make you a valuable asset in an agent position. You have people skills and intuition. Those combined with your legal skills are a lethal cocktail."

I had to admit, I was relieved that he had good reasons to want to hire me, but I was still wary. The perks were appealing, the location ideal and as much as I loved straight law, the position sounded like a lot of fun. I just wasn't sure I could handle having him as my boss. It would've been hard enough if I'd been in the legal department under Mr. Duncan, but now Mr. Ricci was saying he'd be training me directly.

"You have nothing to lose," he said. "Give it a week and if you don't like it, start looking somewhere else. No hard feelings."

I closed my eyes. Carrie's advice floated back to me. If I turned him down without at least trying, I'd never be able to stop wondering 'what if.'

"Okay."

"Excellent."

I could almost hear the smug smile.

"You start on Monday."

"Wait, I can't," I protested. "I have to put in a notice, give Mimi time–"

"I've already taken care of it," he said. "You'll spend today and tomorrow dividing up your work and getting other associates and paralegals up to speed. I expect to see you in my office at eight a.m. first thing next week."

"Oh, okay." I wasn't sure what I was supposed to say to that. "I'll see you then, Mr. Ricci."

"It's DeVon," he said before the call ended.

I sat, staring at the phone for almost a full minute. DeVon. What the hell had I gotten myself into?

FOURTEEN

KRISSY

Sunday morning came much too fast. I was eager to start my new job, but there had been so much to do between Thursday morning when I'd accepted the offer and the day my flight left. And, of course, the hardest of all of it was saying good-bye to Carrie.

We'd already been planning to spend Friday night and all day Saturday together, then start moving her things on Sunday so that Monday after work, she'd go straight to Gavin's place. Correction, I thought, her and Gavin's place. Now our last weekend together had not only been spent finishing her packing but doing mine as well. The sight of our apartment looking bare had bothered me more than I'd thought it would.

I made sure I kept up a cheerful conversation as Carrie drove me to the airport, but I didn't think she was fooled. I was trying very hard not to cry. Her eyes were already shining with tears when she parked the car and turned towards me.

"I can't believe you're leaving," Carrie said. "For the past six years, no matter what's happened, I've known I could count on you."

"You can still count on me," I said.

"But it's not the same," she replied. "It was going to be weird enough to be moving four blocks away and not seeing you at work, but at least you would've been close enough that if I needed you, you were right there."

"And if you need me, I'll be back here in a heartbeat." Tears were burning against my eyelids. "Night or day, if you need me, call and I'll come."

Her tears spilled over and she grabbed me in a fierce hug. I squeezed my eyes shut as I hugged her back, telling myself that I'd promised not to cry. If I cried, it'd just make her cry harder, and I'd never leave. Carrie had been my best friend, my sister, from the moment she'd walked into our dorm room, all mousey and quiet with her Southern accent. And now everything was changing.

Reluctantly, I pulled back. "I have to go. I can't miss my plane... again."

She chuckled and sniffled, wiping the backs of her hands across her cheeks. "I'll make sure the movers don't drop anything when they come tomorrow."

"I just hope I have an apartment by the time they get to LA," I said, trying for a smile. "Living out of a moving truck probably isn't as glamorous as it sounds."

I got the smile I wanted.

"Gavin and I will come visit soon," Carrie said.

"You better." I gave her a wicked grin. "I would say if you don't, I'd have to come spank you both, but you'd like that."

Carrie's face turned bright red. "I never should have told you about that."

Before the mood could get serious again, I climbed out of the car and pulled my bag out of the backseat. This one was bigger than the one I'd taken before since I knew I'd be at least four or five days without the rest of my wardrobe. I was going to be making a lot, but I didn't have it now to spend on extra clothes.

I spent most of the flight trying to plan what I was going to do when I landed, but every time I started, another memory from my time in New York would make its way forward, reminding me of what I was leaving behind.

The time Leslie, Dena, Carrie and I had crashed a wedding at some museum. Carrie would've remembered which one. What I remembered was the four of us running from the security guards, carrying our heels and laughing so hard we almost got caught. That had been my idea, a dare for Leslie that had somehow turned into all four of us doing it.

Meeting Leslie and Dena for the first time.

The nights we'd stay in eating ice cream and watching chick-flicks.

Getting a call at two in the morning from a broken-hearted Dena when her high school sweetheart died in a car accident. We'd all gone and stayed with her for two days.

The Fridays after work when we'd go to a bar or club to unwind after a long week.

Forcing Carrie to go talk to the hottie at the bar, and then seeing how happy she was with him.

By the time I arrived at LAX, I was emotionally wrung out. No one was waiting for me this time, which wasn't surprising since I hadn't told anyone when I was coming in, but I was glad. I didn't want to have to pretend to put on a happy face, even for a company driver.

I stood with everyone else who was trying to get a cab and when I got in, I gave the driver the address to Hotel Hollywood. I'd considered going back to the hotel where the company had put me up, but they cost three hundred and fifty dollars a night, even in their least expensive room. Since I wasn't sure how many nights I was going to stay, I'd opted for something nice, but less expensive. My first paycheck wouldn't be coming until the end of the month, and while that would take care of any financial issues, right now I only had my savings, which was enough for a deposit and the first couple months' rent.

I hadn't really had time to start looking at places, but at least the cost didn't seem too much different than New York. Back home – back in the city, I corrected myself – I'd needed a roommate because I hadn't been making enough to afford a place of my own. Here, with my much larger salary, I could afford it, but I didn't know if I wanted to. I'd never lived alone. I'd gone from my parents' house to rooming with Carrie at Columbia to rooming with her in our apartment. I was afraid that living by myself would be too quiet.

Maybe I'd find a two bedroom and then start looking for someone who wouldn't mind my mess. Maybe I could even offer a lower portion of the rent if she kept the place clean. That way, I wouldn't need to worry about it or have to feel guilty for not doing it. I allowed myself a small smile. That was a brilliant idea.

The hotel was nice, nothing too fancy, but not some one-night place that people traveling used as a place to sleep before moving on. I could be comfortable here while I looked for apartments over the next couple days. My stuff would arrive probably on Wednesday or Thursday, and I didn't want to have to rent a storage unit, so I'd probably be spending the rest of the day looking for places to visit after work tomorrow.

I didn't really have much to unpack, but by the time I was done, I was starving. I'd been so worked up this entire weekend, I hadn't eaten a lot. I wasn't sure if Sunset Plaza was close enough to walk to, but I could get a cab. I frowned. I didn't want to risk running into Taylor. He'd been polite when we'd parted ways, but that had been before I'd found out that he'd been paid to flirt with me. I wasn't sure how I'd react if I saw him.

Fortunately, I'd spotted a small café down the street when I'd arrived. That looked as good a place as any. After the long flight, I was glad to stretch my legs and I let myself enjoy the late afternoon sunshine, reminding myself of the gray skies in New York when I'd left.

As I walked, for the first time, I noticed the homeless people begging on the sidewalk. Being from Chicago and New York, this wasn't exactly something I hadn't seen before. Here, it made a bit more sense than it did in either of those other cities. Here, at least, the weather was almost always nice, plus there were plenty of tourists. I usually limited my interactions to working soup kitchens around the holidays, but today, I dropped a five dollar bill into the box that sat in front of an older man. He had a large beard and a long, thin face. He kind of looked like a guy I'd seen playing Jesus on a movie once.

"Go get yourself some lunch," I said with a smile.

"God bless you, child," he said as he picked up the bill.

I continued on my way, occasionally dropping some change and a couple one dollar bills as I went. I knew I couldn't afford to do this every day, and I couldn't give all of them five dollars, but at least I could help a little. By the time I reached the café, the smile was staying and I was feeling much better. I still missed New York and my friends, but I could see a good life here. A new job. A new place. New friends.

DeVon's face flashed through my mind.

A new boss.

My stomach clenched. There was that, too. A new boss who pissed me off... and maybe turned me on.

My phone rang, interrupting my less-than-welcomed thoughts. I looked down at the screen. Mom. Damnit. I'd been ignoring her calls all weekend. I hadn't told her about my interview in LA and I had no clue how to tell her that I'd already moved here. DeVon had said to give it a week, but I knew the chances of me quitting were slim. Jensens didn't quit.

I sighed. I had to talk to her sometime, and at least a conversation with her would distract me from what I'd been thinking.

"Hey, Mom."

"Krissy Marie Jensen, have you been avoiding my calls?"

I winced. Mom didn't yell or even raise her voice. When she

was pissed, her voice got quieter. She was barely speaking above a whisper right now.

"I'm sorry, Mom. I've been really busy with work." That, at least, was the truth.

"You and your father," she said. "Sometimes I wonder how he ever found the time to contribute to your conception."

I closed my eyes and resisted the urge to say that the last thing I wanted to think about over a meal was my conception.

"I tried calling him to see what you were up to, but he didn't even take my call. Some big new case, I supposed. Amelia said I was being too sensitive. She always says I'm too sensitive."

And now we'd moved from complaining about my father to complaining about her newest lover. My mom had 'discovered herself' when I was about eleven or twelve, but she and my dad managed to hold it together until I was thirteen. Sometimes I thought it was because he was usually so busy with his law firm that it had taken him that long to realize that his wife was a lesbian. Not that I'd ever asked. That was one of my top "conversations to never have with my parents."

"So, darling, I need to know if you're planning on coming home for Thanksgiving. Your father will be working, I assume, but Amelia wants to bring her parents over to meet you."

I didn't mention that I'd never met Amelia myself. The last of my mother's girlfriends I'd met had been Summer, and that had been six months and two lovers ago. My mom's a bit high-maintenance. Not in the money sense, because she had all the money. When your dad's a big-shot lawyer pulling in six figures easy and he's the 'poorer' parent, that's saying something. Mom was old money. Her great-great-grandfather, or something like, that had struck gold or oil and moved the family up in society. At least, that was the story the family told. I personally suspected we were descended from some gangsters who'd gotten rich during Prohibition and then invested wisely. Again, a conversation to avoid.

"Krissy?" My mom repeated my name.

"Sorry, Mom," I mumbled. "I don't know if I'm going to be able to make it home for Thanksgiving."

"And why not?" Back to her quiet voice.

"Because I have a new job, and I don't know what days I get off."

"Honey, the flight's only a couple hours, and I'd be happy to pay for it."

"I don't want your money, Mom," I said the sentence automatically. I'd been saying it since I'd graduated from high school. My parents had insisted on paying for college, and that wasn't one I argued about much, but everything else had been me. I didn't want anyone saying I'd gotten to where I was riding my parents' coattails, and I didn't want anyone trying to suck up to me just because my parents were rich. "And it's not a couple hours."

"Sure it is."

I took a deep breath. "My new job's in LA, Mom. I'm not in New York anymore."

"Excuse me?"

Wow. That was the quietest I'd ever heard her. "I took a job in LA. In fact, I just moved out here today."

"Does your father know about this?"

My parents had stayed mostly amicable after the divorce, but things tended to get a little ugly if I told Dad something and not Mom. Dad didn't care. He was happy with what I gave him, when I gave it, and concentrated on his work the rest of the time. I wasn't sure which annoyed me more.

"No, Mom. It happened really fast."

"You know," she said. "If you'd take your father's job offer at his firm, you'd never have to worry about vacations."

"I want to make it on my own," I argued.

"And you've proven that you can," she countered. "But one day you're going to inherit my portion of the family money and take your place as the public face of our family. You need to come home so you can be properly trained."

More training. I wondered if DeVon's training would include the rigorous etiquette lessons and ass-kissing that my mom's lessons would have. It was possible.

"Mom." I kept my tone firm. "I love you and I love Dad, but I'm doing this. Now, I have to go look for an apartment. I'll let you know closer to Thanksgiving if I'll be home, and I'll definitely try to make it out for Christmas."

"Krissy..."

"Love you, Mom."

I hung up before she could say anything else. I loved my parents, but they were a handful. One of the reasons I hadn't stayed in Chicago for school had been to get away from them. We got along much better when we were apart. Dad didn't feel guilty and I didn't resent him. Mom could focus on herself and she couldn't control me.

I paid my bill and headed back to the hotel. I was more determined than ever not to quit, no matter how asinine DeVon's behavior. I had to prove to my parents that this was the right choice. I didn't even want to think about the alternative.

FIFTEEN

KRISSY

I was actually relieved when I saw that my office was about average-sized. It wasn't as big as some of the ones I'd passed coming in, but it wasn't tiny either. I'd been afraid I was going to end up in this massive corner office and really piss some people off. I was there to work, but I hoped I'd at least make a couple friends, like I'd done at Webster and Steinberg. I already felt like I didn't deserve the job. I didn't need anything else to make me stand out.

Once the relief passed, I was able to sit behind my desk and appreciate everything. The décor was modern like the rest of the building – with the exception of DeVon's office. The office chair I sat on was comfortable enough that I knew it cost more than I'd made in a month in New York. The two chairs on the other side of the desk looked just as expensive. There were no paintings or anything on the walls and I made a mental note to try to find something to make it feel more personable in here. The outside wall and front wall were glass, and I supposed that was a good thing. I knew people were probably going to be talking about me. If DeVon came in to see me, at least there'd be no gossip about what we were doing behind my closed doors. I wondered how many of the women out there had experienced the same unique interviews I had.

I turned to my computer and pushed thoughts of DeVon and his women out of my head. I was here to work. I had to prove that I deserved this office instead of being downstairs among the cubicles with the rest of the legal department.

"Excuse me, Ms. Jensen?" A pretty, red-haired girl knocked on my open door.

"Yes?"

"Hi," she said brightly. "I'm Tracy, your PA."

I couldn't help but smile back. She reminded me a little of Leslie when we'd first met, fresh out of college, just turned twenty-one. "It's nice to meet you, Tracy, and please, call me Krissy." If I was going to call DeVon by his first name, then Tracy could call me by mine.

"Krissy, then." Her smile widened and she came into the office. She was dressed in a cute dress that was the perfect combination of professional and fun. Definitely like Leslie.

"So, DeVon told me to help you get set up," Tracy said.

I felt a pang of disappointment that I wasn't the only employee to use his first name, then I pushed it aside. I had to focus.

Tracy walked around the desk so that she was standing near my computer. Her tone changed to something more brisk and business-like as she turned on the computer. She handed me a slip of paper and, when the login screen came up, she punched in my user information. Passwords would change on a weekly basis and were all randomly generated so that no one could hack the system by guessing that you always used the name of your first crush. I listened carefully as she explained the various programs I would need to access and the uses for each. I'd never been the most computer-savvy of the people working at Webster and Steinberg, but I was smart enough to be able to memorize things.

"I also have these for you." Tracy handed me two files I hadn't seen her bring in. "DeVon sent them to me at the end of last week and said that they're your first two clients." She gave me another charming smile and then headed back out to her own desk.

I picked up the files with a combination of dread and relief. I'd had a hard time sleeping last night, thinking I'd be spending most of my day sitting around with nothing to do. I didn't handle downtime well. I was terrified I'd screw something up, but at least it was work.

I opened the first file and glanced at it, then did the same to the second. Both were female actresses who'd had several small appearances on television shows I didn't watch, but neither one was working now. I'd never seen either one before. I set down the second file and began to read the first more thoroughly.

I was halfway through when Tracy knocked again. "Unless the door's closed," I said. "You don't have to knock."

"Understood." Tracy held out another file.

"More clients?" I wasn't sure why DeVon would be giving me another before I'd done anything with these.

Tracy shook her head. "No, this is the latest 'who's looking' list."

"The what?" I hated looking ignorant, but better I get the information from my PA than risk looking like an idiot in front of some higher-up.

"It's a list of upcoming television and movie projects that are looking for talent, and it also has upcoming auditions." The fact that Tracy answered me without any surprise that I didn't know told me that DeVon had told her about my inexperience in the field. I wasn't sure yet if that was a good thing or bad.

I glanced at the file. It made sense, I supposed. A big part of my job was probably matching my clients with suitable jobs.

"Oh, there's more," Tracy said.

More? I watched Tracy walk out and pick up a huge box that had been sitting on the floor next to her desk.

"DeVon told me to give you this, too."

"What is it?" I almost didn't want to know. The sheer size of the box was intimidating.

"Screenplays." Tracy reached inside and pulled out a sheaf of paper. "Some might make it to a movie, most won't. The trick is to pick a winner. Find something that could work for one of our clients. More than one, if we're really lucky."

I stood and peered into the box. It was full. It would take me months to read all of these. At least I didn't have to worry about being bored.

"By the way, we get a box like that every week."

I looked up and Tracy was grinning at me, as if she knew I was currently asking myself what I'd gotten into.

"Let me know if there's anything you need." Tracy went back out to her desk.

My eyes returned to the box and I took a deep breath. The best way to deal with a project that seemed overwhelming was to just do it. I began to unload the box, making neat piles on my desk, separating by genre.

I'd only been working for a couple minutes when someone knocked on my door. I raised my head to remind Tracy she didn't need to knock and saw a man standing in the doorway. He looked like he was at least ten to fifteen years older than me, which meant if he was like most of Hollywood, he was closer to twenty years older and had gotten work done.

"Sorry to disturb." When he smiled, he flashed teeth far too white to be natural. "I'm your new neighbor." He pointed at the office to the right of mine. "George Hamilton, no relation to the actor." His laugh made me want to squirm, and not in a good way.

"Hi." I forced a smile and walked over to him, holding out my hand. "I'm Krissy Jensen. It's nice to meet you."

"I have to ask," he said. "There are a few of us who are very curious about something. In fact, we have a bet going and need you to settle it."

I had a feeling I wasn't going to like where this was going.

He grinned at me with those obscenely white teeth. "What exactly did you have to do to land this job?"

"Excuse me?" My question was flat. He couldn't mean what I thought he meant.

"You know," he said. "What 'favors' did you have to provide to get hired for this kind of position?"

The pleasant mask had slipped a bit, and I could see in his eyes that he thought I was nothing more than a high-priced whore.

My mouth tightened and I could hear blood rushing in my ears. "You want to know if I had to do more than blow the boss to earn this?" I could tell my blunt question startled him. Most women probably got all embarrassed or defensive. I wasn't about to do either. I took a step towards him. "Is that what you're asking, George? You want the details, right? So you can get off picturing it later?"

That smile faltered and I saw a flash of anger.

"You want to know if I fucked him? Let him bend me over his desk? Take it up the ass? Use me like a whore?" I was just a few inches from him now and the scent of his cologne was almost over-whelming. "I don't suppose it ever occurred to you that a woman could be hired for more than a nice pair of tits and a tight ass."

"I-I..." he stammered.

I didn't let him say anything else. "Don't worry. I'm not going to report you for sexual harassment. I don't need HR to send you to some bullshit sensitivity training. What I am going to do is make sure that you and the rest of the assholes who think I fucked my way into this job regret it, by making you all look completely worth-less to this company." I took a step back. "Now get the fuck out of my office. I'm sure you have some ass-kissing to do."

It wasn't until he left that I felt my nails biting into my palms. My hands were actually shaking, I was so pissed. I'd been afraid this would happen, that people would assume I'd slept with DeVon for the job. That just made me want to work twice as hard to prove that I could not only do this but excel at it. I might've gone a bit too far with George, but I knew his type. He was the kind of guy who'd take embarrassment or outright denial as an admission of guilt because he didn't believe there was any way a woman could be hired because she was better for the job than he was.

I just hoped I was as good as I'd made myself out to be.

It took me a couple minutes to regain my composure as I finished sorting the files. I kept my eyes on my work, not wanting to look out and see if Tracy had heard the confrontation. I really didn't want to be labeled the company bitch. When I did risk a glance up, she was watching me and gave me a thumbs-up. That was enough to tell me that most of the employees, at least the female ones, thought George was a dick too.

I'd just reached the bottom of the box when my phone rang. That was surprising, since I'd assumed my calls would come through Tracy. I picked it up.

"Krissy."

My insides twisted at the way my name sounded coming from DeVon. I couldn't stop myself from wondering what it would sound like in bed, heated with passion.

"Yes?" I nearly squeaked and my face burned.

"I have a lunch with an executive from Universal Pictures, and I'd like you join me."

I knew it would piss off some people if I got to go to a business lunch with the boss and some big-wig from Universal, but it was too good of an opportunity to pass up. I wanted to succeed at this job now more than ever, just to prove to everyone that I could do it.

"Of course," I said before I could second-guess it.

"Meet me at the restaurant ten minutes early so we can go over a few things. Tracy can give you the address and directions," he said. "You do have a car, right?"

"No," I admitted. "Not yet. I'm going to look for one this week. Until then, it's cabs."

"But you know how to drive?"

"Of course." I would've been annoyed at the question but I knew too many New Yorkers who'd never bothered to learn.

Assuming that I'd know would've been even ruder than the blunt question.

"Take one of the company cars, then. Tell Tracy to get the keys for you."

"Okay, Mr. Ric-I mean, DeVon. I'll see you there."

I didn't get a response because the line was already dead. He hung up before I'd finished speaking.

Like I'd said before. Asshole.

SIXTEEN

KRISSY

I really liked the BMW Tracy gave me the keys for. It handled like a dream. Like most company cars, it was black, but I wondered what it would look like cherry red. Maybe I'd look into one for myself.

I handed the keys to the valet as I walked past him into Spago's, one of the most famous restaurants in Beverly Hills. I had a feeling this was one of those places that took reservations a year ahead of time unless you had connections. I was wagering DeVon had connections.

"Krissy."

His voice drew my attention and the pretty woman who was waiting to seat me motioned me to go ahead. I walked slowly, hoping I looked calmer than I felt. I was wearing a simple black dress since, on my first day, I didn't want to look too flashy or too dowdy, but now I wasn't so sure that had been the right choice. The way DeVon's eyes ran down my body, then back up again, told me he approved.

He stood as I approached and pulled out a chair. He then

kissed first one cheek, then the other. It shouldn't have surprised me considering the faint Italian accent that told me he hadn't been born here, but I hadn't been expecting the heat from his lips against my skin, and it was all I could do to keep from shivering.

I sat and hoped my face wasn't red. DeVon didn't seem to notice anything off as he handed me a menu. I wondered if it would be inappropriate for me to order something alcoholic. I really wanted a drink. I refrained, however, and just asked for water. I had a feeling DeVon wasn't someone I wanted to let my guard down with.

"We're meeting Jake Morris," DeVon began. "He's the second or third most powerful executive at Universal, depending on which of the top three you ask."

I gave a half-smile.

"Here," he said as he gestured around us, "is where the big deals are made. Forget those lists that tell you who's looking for what. No star gets hired that way. It's all about connections. You bring someone like Jake here, you charm him and convince him that he needs your client. That is how stars are made."

It came as no surprise that, in Hollywood, it was more about who you knew than how talented you were. There weren't many places where that wasn't true.

"You have a fire inside you, Krissy." DeVon's voice grew quieter. "And that is a good thing, but that must be tempered in situations such as this. You must charm these people, not insult them." One side of his mouth tipped up in a crooked smile. "Not all of them find a smart mouth to be as...appealing as I do."

I was saved from having to figure out a response to that when DeVon suddenly stood. I did the same.

"Jake." DeVon was all business now.

I was smoothing down my skirt, so I didn't see Jake until I was reaching for his hand. I had to admit, he wasn't anything like what I'd been expecting. You hear Universal Pictures executive and you think three-piece suit and a haircut that cost more than a car.

Jake appeared to be in his forties and looked like he'd spent most of his youth in a 'peace, love, hope' movement. His hair was long, and he had it pulled back in a ponytail. He wore a suit that was obviously tailored to his slender body, but the clothes had a relaxed, almost rumpled look. Now I didn't feel so underdressed.

"I must say, DeVon," Jake said as we all sat down. "When you said you were bringing someone new, I wasn't expecting to see someone so young and beautiful."

I gave him a smile. "Thank you. And when DeVon said we were meeting an executive from Universal, I definitely wasn't expecting anyone like you." I gave him my most charming smile.

"Disappointed?" he asked, raising an eyebrow.

"Not at all." I sipped at my water.

When the waiter came over, we ordered. Everything looked delicious, but there weren't any prices. I didn't want to look like I was trying for the most expensive thing on the menu simply because it was a business lunch, so I stuck with something that looked simple, but appetizing. Smoked Jidori Chicken, wild field mushrooms and Yukon Potato Puree. After Jake and DeVon ordered – pizza with house-made Lamb Merguez sausage, roasted peppers and Cippolini onions for Jake, and a prime ribeye steak with glazed carrots, radishes and Armagnac-Peppercorn sauce for DeVon – we carried on with the small talk.

Or, I should say, Jake and I carried on with the small talk. DeVon said very little as Jake openly flirted with me, and I smiled graciously and answered his questions. He never got too personal, but he made it clear he found me attractive. This, apparently, was how the game was played. And I was good at it.

"So a Columbia graduate with a law degree," Jake sounded impressed. "Looks and brains. You hit the jackpot with this one, DeVon."

He smiled, but I couldn't tell if it reached his eyes.

"What do you think, Krissy? Could I steal you away from Mirage?" Jake asked. His fingers brushed mine as he reached for cream to put into his third cup of coffee. "I'd treat you so much better than DeVon."

"That's very tempting," I said. "I'll keep it in mind for when my week's up. After all, I've been told that if I don't like my job at the end of the week, I can quit, right?" I looked at DeVon, waiting to see if I got any reaction.

He gave me a slight nod and took a sip of his red wine.

"I'm surprised you'd ever consider letting her go," Jake said. He let his eyes run over me. His gaze was just short of being overly friendly. It was enough to let me know that he was only partially teasing and that, if I said the word, he'd take me to bed, but not so much that I felt like I needed a shower afterwards.

"Any dessert?" the waiter asked as he cleared a few empty plates.

All three of us refused. I wasn't sure I'd be able to finish what was in front of me.

Jake leaned back in his chair and folded his hands over his stomach. "I think that's your cue to talk about the reason for your invitation, DeVon. I know you didn't bring me here for my wit."

DeVon didn't deny it or try to sugarcoat it. I liked that.

"You're casting for a new action movie and I want Jason Cooke to star in it."

Jake chuckled. "I hope you like blunt and straightforward, Krissy, because your boss always tells it like it is."

"Jason's a rising star," DeVon continued without acknowledging Jake's comment to me. "He just needs a shot at carrying a film."

Jake rubbed his chin as if he were considering it. "I don't know. The role calls for someone a bit older than Cooke. We're thinking the James Bond type."

"But isn't James Bond a sex symbol?" I angled myself so I was facing Jake. "You want someone with charisma, good looks and that special something that makes women weak in the knees."

Jake nodded, letting me go on.

"Jason has that, plus the acting chops to give him that maturity." I slowly uncrossed and re-crossed my legs. "You'll get the older women drooling over the forbidden fruit, younger ones who can ogle without feeling like they have a daddy complex, and he's a man's man that guys will relate to." I leaned forward slightly and watched Jake's eyes flick down to my breasts, then back up again. "DeVon wouldn't have suggested Jason if he didn't think our client could deliver."

"I'm still not sure," Jake said, but I could tell he was wavering. "We were thinking of getting a big name to headline."

"I'm sure your movie is brilliant enough to draw a crowd with someone who isn't quite as famous as one of your blockbusters." I took a sip of water, and licked the excess moisture off of my lips, knowing it'd draw Jake's attention to my mouth. "Put a clip in the trailer of Jason Cooke without a shirt, and you'll get plenty of people coming for the eye candy alone."

Jake laughed again. "She's good," he said to DeVon. He drained his coffee and stood. "All right. I'll take a sit down with the kid." He looked at DeVon. "And he better be as good as she just made him out to be."

"He is," DeVon said as he stood and reached for Jake's hand.

When Jake shook my hand, he lingered a bit longer than necessary, but not long enough to make me uncomfortable. He was really good at walking that line.

"I look forward to seeing you again."

"Likewise." I smiled as I watched him go. I glanced at my phone. "I should probably be getting back if I have any hope of getting through those manuscripts."

"You did well," DeVon said. He leaned down and scrawled something onto what I assumed was the bill. "And you're right. We should return to the office."

We walked out to where the valets were waiting. They went to get our cars, leaving us standing on the sidewalk, an awkward silence between us.

"I am having a party at my house Friday night," he said suddenly. "You should come."

I stared at him, unable to hide my surprise at the invitation. What the hell was he playing at?

He held up his hands, palms out. "Strictly business. After the way you handled yourself in there, I think you should attend. Jake will be there and we can solidify any details if he hasn't contacted me about meeting with Jason. There'll also be a few other casting directors there, along with some of our biggest clients. Including Jason Cooke." His eyes sparkled.

"I should probably know what he looks like since I was talking him up, right?" I smiled. I'd wondered if he'd realized I'd been skirting the truth, making it seem like I'd known Jason when I didn't.

"You were very careful to never say anything that was an outright lie," DeVon said. "Everything was an implication. That was very much a lawyer thing to do."

I shrugged. "You know what they say about taking the girl out of the city, right?"

"So you will come?"

I hesitated. I wanted to go, partially because it'd be good for my career, but also because I was curious to see how DeVon handled a room.

"You can even bring a friend."

"Okay," I said, unable to conceal how excited I was. I had absolutely no idea who I'd bring, but if I had to, I'd go alone. I wasn't going to do anything that could screw this up for me.

"Excellent," he said. He gave me a once-over. "It's semi-formal, so wear something similar to that, but not in black. I'd like to see you in something with color."

And with that statement, he climbed into his car and left me wondering what he'd meant, if it had been my boss telling me a way to dress for clients...or something else.

SEVENTEEN

KRISSY

I was pleasantly surprised at how quickly I settled into a routine at Mirage. Tracy was a tremendous asset and made sure I knew what I needed to know. Client lists, protocol, filing systems. She was so good at it, I wondered why she wasn't an agent herself.

I met other colleagues, some of whom were as welcoming as Tracy, but a few who still gave me dirty looks that I assumed meant they thought I was sleeping with DeVon. George, at least, had kept his distance. I still saw him every once in a while, shooting glares in my direction, but he never approached me, so I was fine with it.

At the end of the week, I scheduled my first client meetings. I hadn't yet met with either woman in person, but I'd been doing some work on their behalf, calling places, pulling strings, and I had good news for both. At least, I hoped they'd take it as good news. There was always the chance that either or both thought they were above the auditions I'd booked, but everything I'd heard about them both had been good.

Cami Matthews was a petite, delicate-looking blonde in her

late twenties but could easily pass for eighteen. I'd gotten her an audition for a small role as a victim on a well-known crime show, a network television drama for the part of the free-spirited middle sister, and a movie based off of a book about nuclear war where she'd play the little sister to the main character.

Lena Dunn was a tall, striking brunette with caramel-colored skin. She was older than Cami by six years, but she actually looked like an adult, so there were no college roles for her. I'd found her auditions for a small role as a reporter in what would probably be a summer blockbuster, a romantic comedy for the role of the bitchy new girlfriend, and a guest role on a cable medical show where she'd play a nurse who was having an affair with a doctor.

In both meetings, I introduced myself and then presented them with their auditions. When Cami squealed with delight and launched herself from her chair to hug me, I felt a lot better about my work. I didn't expect the same reaction from Lena, and while I didn't get a squeal and a hug, Lena did thank me profusely, telling me that she'd just about given up hope of ever getting another job.

By the time Lena left, I was on cloud nine. Part of me wished the front walls to my office weren't glass, because I would've done a happy dance right there. As it was, I couldn't stop from grinning.

"I'm guessing that smile on your face means that things went well," Tracy said as she came into my office with a small box of what I assumed were manuscripts. She set them on the edge of my desk, next to the slowly dwindling pile already there.

"They were both excited about the auditions," I said as I sat back down behind my desk. "I was worried they wouldn't think the parts were big enough or they'd be mad that I couldn't just get them a role."

Tracy gave me the smile I'd come to know meant I'd shown my ignorance of the industry. "Trust me, even the big-name stars have to at least do a read through for a studio quite often. Getting them each three auditions after only having their files for a week, and none of the parts were commercials...that's a big deal. Not many of our agents could manage that."

As Tracy left, the first thought that came to me was that I couldn't wait to tell Carrie. And then I remembered that Carrie was settling into her new job and her new place just as much as I was. She was probably busy right now. If I'd been in New York, I would've just called and told her to meet me for lunch so we could share stories. A pang of homesickness went through me.

I needed to do something to celebrate, or I was just going to keep thinking about how I wished I could tell Carrie about how well things had gone. I glanced at the clock. It was almost time for lunch. That would be my treat, I decided. I would go back to that amazing restaurant in Sunset Plaza. The weather was beautiful. Having a salad and sandwich on the patio would be a perfect way to reward myself for a job well done.

I was looking over the menu when I heard someone say my name. I looked up and saw the last person I wanted to see at the moment.

"Krissy, I've been trying to get ahold of you."

I was about to ask Taylor if he was stalking me, but then I realized that he was wearing a uniform. He wasn't staking the place out, hoping I'd come for lunch. He worked here.

"Look, Taylor, I just want my lunch." All of the good feelings I'd had about my morning evaporated. I didn't want a reminder of what DeVon had done.

"Please, Krissy, let me explain," he pleaded. His blue eyes were wide and sad. I couldn't say no.

"You've got two minutes," I said.

"DeVon promised that Mirage would sign me, take me on as a client if I took the role, but now he won't even talk to me. And he did more than ignoring me. He must have made some calls or something because I can't get anything now, not even as an extra in a cheap commercial."

I gave him an expectant look, waiting for him to finish. I felt bad that DeVon had screwed up his career, but I couldn't forgive him for the part he'd played in the deception.

"Look, Krissy," he continued. "You have to understand that it was a part I was told to play, but when I met you...the attraction is real. I was just supposed to flirt and see if you took the bait, but I fell for you. I was a total shit-head for doing this to you, and I understand if you never want to speak to me again, but I needed you to know that, past those first few minutes, I wasn't acting. I really wanted to be with you."

I wasn't entirely sure how to respond to this announcement, so I didn't say anything. Something dark passed over Taylor's face and he started to turn away.

"I'll get someone to swap tables."

"Wait!" I blurted out the word. "It's okay."

He turned back towards me, a cautious hope in his eyes.

"I understand why you did it." And I did. He was doing a job. He didn't know DeVon's full plan, and he hadn't known me. I couldn't say I wouldn't have done the same thing if I'd been in his place.

"So, we're okay?" he asked.

I smiled. That sweet guy I'd first been attracted to was the real Taylor. I was sure of it. What I'd disliked about him had been how pushy he'd been, not taking 'no' for an answer. That could all be explained away by DeVon's instructions.

"We're very okay," I said.

As I gave him my order, an idea popped into my mind. It was perfect because it'd piss DeVon off to no end, getting some vengeance for me and Taylor, and it would be fun. Taylor was hot and liked to have fun, the perfect guy for me to invite to DeVon's party this weekend. Taylor would get the chance to meet with Hollywood big-wigs and DeVon couldn't do anything at the party without looking petty or like he didn't know what his protégé was doing. Plus, it'd be nice to see him off balance for once, because there was no way he'd ever guess I'd bring the guy he'd used to deceive me. And since Taylor wasn't a client of Mirage after all, I wasn't breaking any rules.

"Taylor." I gave him my most charming smile. "How would you like to come to a party with me tonight?"

EIGHTEEN

KRISSY

Tracy had given me the keys to a different BMW and I actually liked this one better. A little bigger than the other one, it had a more elegant feel. I was definitely leaning towards buying this model for myself. I'd never been a woman who was impressed by flashy cars, but I did like driving this one.

I left my hotel room with plenty of time to get to Taylor's house, giving me the opportunity to scope out apartments on his side of the city. I still hadn't found one I liked yet. The moving van with my things had broken an axle in Nebraska, so it wouldn't arrive until Monday – they were knocking a third of my bill off so I wasn't going to complain – and I planned on spending the weekend looking for a place. I wasn't quite sure what I was looking for, but I'd know it when I saw it.

Taylor was waiting outside when I pulled up and he was looking very nice in his black suit and tie. I'd done as DeVon had asked and gone with something other than black. I'd been tempted to have Carrie ship me my green 'ribbon' dress just to see what reaction I could get out of DeVon, but I'd decided against it. I still needed to seem professional. My dress had a modest enough neckline and hemline to be considered professional, but hugged my curves enough to draw admiration. Its emerald color was a nice contrast with my skin-tone.

"You look amazing," Taylor said as he climbed into the passenger's side of the car.

"So do you." I smiled at him before starting back down the road. I hadn't been paying close attention the last time I'd gone to DeVon's, so I concentrated on following my GPS, making small talk until we reached the house.

If Taylor was surprised to see where we were, he didn't show it. Instead, he hurried around to my side of the car to open the door and help me out. I handed off the keys to the valet and slipped my arm through Taylor's before heading up through the gates.

DeVon was standing near the entrance and his eyes met mine. His gaze flickered over my outfit and I saw approval for a split second before he registered who was standing at my side. Mister Big-Shot actually faltered, his face hardening. His mouth flattened into a thin line, and I saw the anger flash across his eyes. All of this happened in just a few seconds, and no one who wasn't watching him closely would've seen it.

Before anyone else could notice, he had his professional smile on again and was coming towards Taylor and me.

"Krissy, Taylor." He held out his hand, first to me and then to Taylor. "Good of you to come."

"Thank you for the invitation." I kept my voice cool and polite, immediately returning my arm to Taylor's once the hand-shaking was done.

"Jason," DeVon called over his shoulder without taking his eyes off of me.

I wanted to squirm under that gaze. I'd had men look at me before and had known that they wanted me, but there was something different about what I was sensing from DeVon, and I couldn't quite place my finger on it. I liked it, though, and I hated myself for liking it.

Fortunately, I didn't have to suffer through it for much longer because a handsome man with dark hair and a winning smile was holding out his hand to me.

"Jason Cooke, meet Krissy Jensen, the newest employee of Mirage Talent and the reason you have a sit-down with Jake Morris on Tuesday."

"Nice to meet you," Jason said.

"You, too," I replied.

"Krissy here is going to make sure Jake keeps his promise." DeVon gave me a pointed look and I knew exactly what he was saying.

I was going to have to keep flirting with Jake. I nodded to let DeVon know that I understood. He motioned with his head and I followed the direction. Jake was standing with a couple men in suits and hadn't yet noticed I was there.

I looked up at Taylor and he nodded. I was suddenly glad I'd brought him. He understood that I couldn't act like we were there together. I had to be available, even if I'd never cross that line with Jake. Taylor knew how the game was played and I was learning fast.

"Mingle," I said softly. "Make connections while I work."

He nodded and released my arm, giving my hand a quick squeeze before he headed off in a direction opposite Jake. I put on my best sultry smile, and made my way over to the executive.

"Krissy!" He sounded pleased to see me. "You're looking exceptionally lovely this evening."

"Not so bad yourself," I said as I accepted his kiss on the cheek. "I was just talking to Jason Cooke, and he's looking forward to speaking with you on Tuesday."

Jake laughed. "Listen to her, gentleman. Business, business."

The other men chuckled, two of them giving me an appreciative once over. The way the other one was checking out Jason told me that it wasn't the dress he didn't like.

"Always business before pleasure," I teased. "But now that's out of the way, which of you gentlemen are going to get me a drink?"

I was surprised at how easy it was to work the room. I was used to the flirting without promising follow-through, keeping it teasing but never stepping over that line into purely sexual, but these weren't men at a club looking for some hot twenty-something to take home. I hadn't been sure I'd be able to pull this off for a second time, but it wasn't much different than what I'd done before.

I made subtle innuendos, kept my remarks light and teasing. I used gestures to draw attention to my mouth and body without being overtly sexual. I didn't touch Jake, but I'd get close, letting my hand rest near his arm without actual contact, and when he tried to touch me, I'd playfully laugh it off. I'd gotten my glass of champagne, but had only sipped at it, needing to stay clear-headed. I had to read every minute expression on Jake's face, make sure I wasn't teasing too much that he'd get angry when he realized I wasn't going to sleep with him, but that I was stroking his ego enough to keep his attention.

When he asked me to dance, I agreed, but kept just out of reach as I led the way to the dance floor. Taylor was already there, dancing with a pretty blonde I'd seen on a toothpaste commercial. We shared, alternating between me dancing with Jake, with Taylor, and then the blonde and I dancing together. She and I weren't as comfortable as Carrie and I were, but it was enough to keep Jake's attention on us. I was able to play it as a tease with both the woman and Taylor, then claim I needed a drink when Jake tried to take over again. I had to make sure I stayed in control of the situation.

When a buxom brunette captured his attention a quarter of an hour later, I politely excused myself. I'd been talking and joking for over two hours and needed some air, but I didn't want it alone. I found Taylor finishing a conversation with a woman I recognized as a character on a drama I watched from time to time. She smiled at me as I grabbed Taylor's hand and pulled him towards the back patio.

It was quieter out here. No one milling around, looking for drinks or kissing ass. This was nice. The breeze was still warm and I knew back in New York, the nights would be starting to cool off as autumn approached. I'd never been anywhere that didn't have definite seasons. Being warm in LA when it was snowing back east was going to be strange.

"Everything okay?" Taylor asked.

I smiled at him. "Fine. I was just thinking about how different LA is than New York or Chicago."

Taylor nodded. "I get it. My first winter out here, I kept waiting to wake up to snow covering the ground."

"Does it ever stop being weird?" I asked.

He grinned. "This is Hollywood, what do you think?"

I laughed, a genuine one instead of the mostly fake ones I'd been using all night.

"I'm really glad you invited me tonight," Taylor said, his tone becoming serious. "And not just because it annoyed DeVon to see me here after he's been trying to ignore me."

"Well, I'm really glad you came." The corners of my mouth tipped up in a half-smile. "And not just because bringing you was a good way to get back at DeVon for using you against me."

"So," Taylor said slowly. "We're both glad to be together because we actually like being together?"

I nodded, feeling the air between us shift. I had a choice to make here. I could diffuse the tension and friend-zone him, or I could give in to the physical attraction I'd had towards him from the first moment I saw him.

He stepped in front of me and slid his hand around the back of my neck, and I knew if I was going to stop him, this was the time to do it.

I let him pull me forward to meet his mouth. I pushed aside any doubts or questions I had and let myself lean into the kiss. My hands slid under his jacket to feel his hard chest and stomach beneath his thin dress shirt as his tongue teased at my mouth. I parted my lips, expecting him to immediately plunge inside, but he surprised me, letting his tongue trace my lips, first the outside, then the inside. I could feel his restraint, his muscles flexing and twitching beneath my palms as he forced himself to keep it slow.

I ran my hands up to his neck, my fingers playing with the short hair at the base. I slid my tongue alongside his, drawing it deeper into my mouth. He groaned, and the hand on the back of my neck slid down to my ass. I pressed myself closer to him, enjoying the feel of his hard body against mine.

The hand not on my ass slid up my hip to the side of my breast and I reluctantly pulled back. Taylor's face was flushed, and we were both panting as we took a step back.

"I think we should call it a night," I said when I finally got back enough breath to speak. "I'll take you home."

Taylor's eyes were a much deeper blue when he looked at me, full of the desire I'd felt in his kiss. He nodded. "That's probably a good idea."

NINETEEN

DEVON

The petite blonde in front of me with the baby blue eyes and tiny dress was one of Mirage's most promising stars. Or at least that's how Kelsee Hawkey had been trying to sell it to me all night. She'd also made it very clear that she was willing to do *anything* to get ahead.

Granted, she was a little younger than my usual conquests, barely over twenty, but she was smoking hot and willing as hell. I should've been setting her up for the kill, but instead, I was barely paying attention to what she was saying and kept stealing glances at Krissy and Jake.

I told myself it was because I was her boss, and I needed to make sure she was doing her job. The only problem with that was the better she did her job, the more it annoyed me. I was pleased she was capturing his attention, giving just enough to keep Jake interested but not so much that she was throwing herself at him. She was as good as I'd hoped.

When she'd first shown up with Taylor – just the thought of him made me clench my jaw – I was pissed. I knew why she'd done it. He'd obviously told her a sob story about how I'd been avoiding his calls and she'd decided to bring him as payback for how I'd deceived her. Once I'd gotten over the initial annoyance at seeing the two of them together, I'd seen the good in it. I could respect her trying to show me up. She certainly knew how to play the game. The fact that she'd been willing to pretend to overlook Taylor's part in the whole thing just to get back at me showed so much promise. Between that and her skillful maneuvering of Jake, I could see that she was going to be a huge asset to my company.

As Krissy moved into her second hour of laughing at Jake's jokes, I tried to focus my attention on Kelsee. I ran my gaze over her, undressing her with my eyes, though there wasn't much to take off. Her nipples were visible through her thin dress, confirming my previous suspicions that she wasn't wearing a bra. I approved of her choice. Her tits were smaller than...some *other* women's, but they were firm and high, perky enough that she didn't need any extra support. I hadn't noticed a pantyline and wondered if she'd forgone those as well.

I entertained myself for a few minutes thinking about Kelsee and her lack of undergarments. How would she react, I wondered, if I pressed her up against a wall and slid my hand beneath her dress? Fingered her into an orgasm right here in the middle of the party? Or, better yet, led her over to a chair and had her sit on my lap, unbuckled my pants and slid right inside her? Of course, I'd never do the latter. It didn't matter if a woman said she'd been tested, gotten a clean bill of health, and was on the pill. I didn't trust them. One time was all it took to get some STD or get a woman pregnant, all because I trusted her.

"So, I told Marcie that if she thought I was going to back down just because she wanted the part, too, she could forget it."

Kelsee's voice drew me back from the unappealing route my thoughts had taken. She had a nice voice. It was sugary sweet, the kind that went with the plaid skirt and white blouse of a school-girl's uniform.

I turned my attention away from Kelsee, searching again for Krissy. Kelsee was hot, no doubt, but I couldn't quite focus. Maybe that was a good thing. This was a business engagement, after all. Granted, I often mixed business with pleasure. Despite my strict rules for my employees regarding dating clients, quite a few of my...conquests came from the pool of actresses who paraded through Mirage's doors. I excused my hypocrisy by telling myself that it was different. Other people, no matter how much they denied it, rarely did the whole sex-only thing. There were always emotions involved. Not with me. I never wanted to date these women. It was fucking, pure and simple. Okay, maybe *pure* wasn't the right word, but it was the right idea.

"Who's she?" Kelsee asked.

"Krissy Jensen," I answered, knowing she'd followed my gaze to find out why I wasn't mesmerized with her. "She's a new employee at Mirage."

"Oh." Kelsee sounded relieved, then impressed. "Is that Jake Morris she's with? Like Universal Pictures Jake Morris?"

"Mm-hm." I made a non-committal noise as I watched Krissy lead Jake to the dance floor.

They headed straight for Taylor who was dancing with some blonde. Krissy was definitely putting effort into her time with Jake. As she started to move, my chest tightened and I couldn't look away. I'd seen hundreds, thousands, of women dance. Some without clothes, some with. Some had even had professional training. But there was something about the way Krissy moved that made me wonder what she would look like in my bed, her naked body against my black silk sheets, her will totally under my control...

"You have an amazing house, Mr. Ricci." Kelsee pressed her body closer to mine, managing to pull my attention from Krissy. Her hand brushed my thigh.

"Thank you," I said. The heat I'd felt when I'd looked at Krissy was fanning into a flame as Kelsee's hand moved from brushing 'accidentally' against me to actually stroking my leg, her fingers moving closer and closer to my groin.

"I'd love a private tour." Kelsee was practically purring.

I smiled at her and took her hand. If she kept up that rubbing, I wasn't going to be able to mingle with the rest of my guests. I pressed my lips to the back of her hand before releasing it. "It's DeVon, and right now I have to go talk to other guests, but if you stay, I promise I'll give you a very *special* private tour later."

"I won't go anywhere," she promised.

I nodded and then turned to make my way through the crowd. I hated the schmoozing part of my job, but the thought of Kelsee and everything I could do to her kept a smile on my face as I made small talk. I was going to take my time with her, make sure she was writhing and begging for everything.

"DeVon!"

I turned and saw Jake coming towards me. I didn't see Krissy. Where the hell had she gone? I hadn't told her how long she needed to stay, and she'd been keeping Jake occupied for a while, but it bothered me that I didn't know where she was.

"You are one lucky son of a bitch," Jake said. "How do you do it? Find someone so smoking hot with so much talent."

I saw a brunette trying to squeeze in beside Jake, the smile on her face telling me exactly what she was going to offer him. I thought she was a fairly new client, maybe one Penny was handling, but I couldn't say for sure.

"Yes, she's very talented." I gave the brunette a polite smile.

Jake looked over at her, then shook his head. He ignored the woman and said, "No, Krissy. She's amazing."

I would've felt bad for the brunette being dismissed like that, but I knew she'd just set her sights on someone else. Sure enough, before I could finish agreeing with Jake, shewas heading towards the bar where several other studio people and casting directors were lingering.

"Do you mind if I take a shot at her?" Jake asked. "I mean, she didn't say she was dating anyone."

My stomach churned at the thought of Jake asking Krissy out on a date. Him kissing her. Her naked body beneath him... "Knock yourself out," I said. I didn't know what was wrong with me today. There wasn't a chance in hell that Krissy would go for Jake. He was not her type.

Out of the corner of my eye, I spotted Krissy heading for the back patio, Taylor following behind her. I quickly excused myself and made my way through the crowd. I told myself I just wanted to speak with her about how things were going with Jake, but I couldn't deny that I was curious about why Taylor was with her. She'd already gotten her little dig in earlier, and then they'd gone their separate ways. True, they'd danced together, but she'd also danced with Jake and a blonde actress I thought was named Hannah.

I slipped outside, careful not to make any noise as I ducked into the shadows. I wasn't close enough to hear what they were saying, but I could see that they were standing close together. That surprised me. She had to be angry at him for his part in my deception, so why was she acting like she was enjoying being here with him when there wasn't anyone around to see?

His hand went around the back of her neck, and I waited for her to pull back, maybe even slap him, but she didn't. Instead, she let him kiss her. And it wasn't just some little peck, meant to convey friendship. When he grabbed her ass, I turned around and went inside. I didn't want to see any more. What I wanted was to find Kelsee and make sure she was staying because I'd lost any doubts I'd had about fucking her tonight.

TWENTY

KRISSY

There was definitely an advantage to the bigger car, I decided. It made what Taylor and I were doing so much easier.

He was a good kisser, using just enough tongue, but not so much that I felt like I was going to choke on it. Not sloppy like some guys I'd been with. He was a bit hesitant with his hands, which surprised me, but that could've been because I'd shot him down so many times before. I could see how that'd mess with a guy's head.

I definitely wasn't going to shoot him down now. The last time I'd had sex, there hadn't been any of this, so it had been a while since I'd made out with someone. Now that he knew I wasn't going to slap his hands away, he was taking full advantage of me half-laying on top of him as we leaned against the door.

His hands slid up over my hips and squeezed my ass before moving up to my breasts. He wasn't touching skin, but I could feel the heat of his palms through my dress and I could only imagine what they would feel like through the even thinner fabric of my panties and bra.

His lips moved down my jaw to my neck and I tipped my head back to give him easier access. An impish part of me wanted to tell him to give me a hickey, just so DeVon could see it, but I didn't. As much as I wanted to annoy my boss, I didn't want to get the reputation of office slut. Enough people were already assuming I was sleeping with DeVon. I didn't need to add fuel to the fire.

I pressed my hips more firmly against Taylor's, and he moaned against my neck. I could feel him hardening against me and wondered what it would look like. Thick and short? Long and thin? Would it curve up towards the firm abs I was currently running my hands over? Did he shave? Wax? Was his chest as smooth as DeVon's?

I gave my head a little shake. I was definitely thinking too much. I just wanted to enjoy the pleasurable heat that was building between us.

"Are you okay?" Taylor asked, apparently distracted by my head shake.

I smiled at him. "Very okay."

He shifted, glancing through the fogged-up window at the little house behind him. It wasn't anything fancy, but it wasn't run-down either. I liked it. Maybe I'd get a house with roommates instead of an apartment.

"Do you want to come in for a drink?" Taylor asked, his tone suggesting that he'd be interested in more than a drink if I was so inclined.

I sighed and pushed myself up. "I don't think I'm ready to meet the roommates."

"They're out of town."

I gave him a skeptical look, and he raised both of his hands, palms out.

"I swear. Some kind of poker tournament in Vegas." He gave me a shy smile. "We'd have the place to ourselves."

The space between my legs throbbed. It had definitely been too long and Taylor *was* hot. I could either go home and get myself off, or I could go inside for a drink and see where things went from there.

I went with option two.

I hadn't drank much at the party since I'd known I had to make sure Jake didn't take things too far, so the drink Taylor offered me was welcomed.

"One of my roommates, Kyle, he's auditioning for a part of a bartender, so he went out and got all of this." Taylor waved his hand over the plethora of bottles on the kitchen counter.

I smiled, but I didn't want to hear about his roommate. I drained my glass and grabbed the front of his shirt, pulling him towards the living room. He followed without complaint, his arms going around my waist as I turned towards him.

His mouth found mine and I could taste the shot of vodka he'd taken. I moved my hands between us, working open the buttons to his dress shirt until I could slip my hand inside. I wasn't sure when he'd taken off his jacket. Maybe around the time I'd abandoned my shoes.

He caught his breath when my nails raked over his nipple, and I felt the flesh harden. The hands on my waist flexed. I pulled us backwards until we tumbled onto the couch, Taylor landing on top of me. He was bigger than me, but not so much that his weight was too much.

Our lips moved together as I tugged his shirt out of his pants and finished unbuttoning it. If he'd been rich, I would've just torn it off, but I knew Taylor didn't have an overabundance of money to buy dress shirts, so I made myself go slow and not tear anything. I did, however, throw it onto the floor without a second thought. I ran my hands all over his back and shoulders, enjoying the way his muscles bunched and flexed under my touch.

He shifted so that he could kiss my jaw, then throat. I made a pleased sound, but I wanted him lower. I took his hand and put it on my bare thigh, hoping he'd take that hint. When he didn't, I moved my body so that his fingers slid under my dress and his mouth met my collarbone.

Almost hesitantly, he nudged the strap of my dress with his nose. I rolled my shoulder, letting the strap fall. He kissed his way across my shoulder and then down along my neckline. I moaned when he finally reached the top of my breasts. The hand on my thigh moved up to my hip, his fingertips brushing against the part of my ass that wasn't covered by my panties.

I sighed. While I liked his touch, he was taking far too long with this. At this rate, we'd both fall asleep before we got to the good stuff. I pressed my lips to his ear and said the magic words.

"Show me your bedroom."

TWENTY-ONE

DEVON

Kelsee was waiting right where I'd left her. A handful of men were around her, flirting and laughing, but as soon as her eyes met mine, I knew she was mine for the night. The men all looked up at me when I approached, parting so that I could get close enough to Kelsee to whisper in her ear.

"Are you staying?"

She nodded, her eyes glowing. She knew exactly what I was asking.

"Good." I took a few steps back and let the ring of men close around her again. It didn't matter what they said to her. She wouldn't be leaving with any of them.

I was tempted to cut the party short. Every muscle in my body was tense and I couldn't quit seeing Krissy and Taylor kissing. His hand on her ass. Her body leaning into his.

I made small talk with all the important people and blew off Jake's question about where Krissy had disappeared to by saying that she'd had a long week and probably wanted to call it a night. I didn't know if he believed me, but I was having a hard time caring.

I wanted to believe my lie. It was feasible enough. I knew she still hadn't found an apartment, which meant she was probably going to spend the weekend looking. That could be exhausting. She probably had taken Taylor home, then went back to the hotel, showered and gone to bed.

I could almost picture her in the shower, the water caressing her body...

I shook my head in a vain attempt to clear it. I shouldn't be thinking about her in the shower or wondering what she wore to bed. Cute little pajamas with something like hearts or butterflies on them? Sexy silk lingerie? Nothing?

Damnit!

I looked at the clock over the fireplace. In about thirty minutes, I could start hinting that the party was coming to an end. I could make it thirty minutes. I glanced over my shoulder at Kelsee and she ran her tongue out along her bottom lip.

The things I was going to do to that mouth.

The next hour was excruciatingly slow. Most people took the hint when I started my 'farewell' rounds, but some were either too drunk or too stupid to figure it out. I ended up having to practically escort a few of them out, one of whom was a very drunk client who managed to grab my dick a couple times before I got him into a taxi. I almost felt bad for him since at least half a dozen reporters who'd been hanging around the gate saw him do it at least once. That was going to be a very awkward coming out.

When I returned from dropping him off, I did a final check in each of the rooms after instructing Kelsee to stay where she was. This wasn't a tour pass, this was to make sure none of my guests had wandered off and passed out in a corner somewhere. The first party I'd had like this, I'd woken up at three in the morning with a very confused red-head who was trying to figure out why I was in her bed. She'd been sober enough to be embarrassed when I'd told her I wasn't in her bed, and sober enough to consent when we'd fucked. While I'd enjoyed that very much – she'd been a screamer

– it wasn't an experience I wanted to repeat. I didn't like surprises. I liked to be in control.

After I'd cleared the last room – the special guest room where Kelsee and I would eventually end up – I went back down to the main room. Kelsee was standing by the bar, a pleased smile on her face. I didn't speak to her as I walked over and poured myself a scotch. Still without a word, I walked over to my favorite armchair and sat down, sipping at the expensive alcohol.

Kelsee walked towards me slowly, putting a swing in her step that would've been a bit more enticing if she'd had some curves, but considering I could see how hard her nipples were beneath her dress, I wasn't going to be picky. She slipped off her shoes, losing enough height to make her over a foot shorter than me. My cock gave an interested twitch. There was something to be said about how exciting it was to be so much more physically overwhelming than someone you were fucking. I usually liked women who felt more...durable, but every once in a while, I enjoyed the ones like Kelsee who appeared so fragile.

She didn't speak, which surprised me, but rather climbed right onto my lap, her movements almost catlike as she rubbed against me. Her ass brushed against my cock, but she didn't settle there. Instead, she settled lower on my thigh and let her hand drop between us. Her fingers danced over the fabric of my pants, teasing me. I wondered if she thought she was the one in control, the one seducing me.

I took another swallow of my scotch. I didn't mind when they started out thinking that way. Sometimes it made the game more exciting as they realized who was truly in charge.

Then her eyes met mine and I knew she had absolutely no doubt who was in control here. Her fingers stroked me more firmly through my pants and my cock started to harden. I had no doubt that she'd follow my every instruction, that she'd let me do what I wanted to her, but not because she thought that was how she was going to get ahead, but because she wanted it, too. She didn't have to say it because it was written on her face. I'd been with enough women to know the difference between one who thought they'd endure whatever was done in order to advance their career, and the ones who craved what I had to offer. It would take only a few seconds to confirm that Kelsee was the latter.

And if she wasn't, I'd call her cab. I didn't fuck women who weren't truly into it.

She lightly squeezed me, smiling as my cock swelled even more. I grabbed her wrist, putting enough pressure on it to make her eyes widen. It didn't hurt, but it got her attention. I set my now empty glass down and slid my free hand under her dress. She didn't stop me as I ran my palm over her hip and then up her side to her breast. I didn't cup it or caress it or anything like that. With my eyes locked on hers, I pinched her nipple between my thumb and forefinger.

She gasped, but it wasn't a sound of pain. I squeezed tighter and twisted. She made a pained sound, and I held it for another moment longer. When I let go and removed my hand, her eyes were even wider than before and she was taking jagged breaths, but she wasn't protesting.

I gave her a nudge and she climbed off my lap. I stood and held out a hand. "Are you ready for that tour now?"

TWENTY-TWO

KRISSY

Taylor was on the bed, already down to his black boxer-briefs, when I finally got out of my dress. The make-out session from the couch had continued in the bedroom and it was clear, now, that I was going to have to take charge. I didn't mind since it usually meant I could get myself off at least once. I'd had a couple guys try to take control completely, but those encounters ended with me with my hand between my legs while the guy was looking for his pants. When it was give and take, the odds of me having an orgasm were better, but not as good as they were when I got to drive.

I unsnapped my bra and let it slide down my shoulders, slowly exposing my breasts. Taylor's eyes darkened when my nipples came into view. The panties went next, and then I was completely naked.

"Your turn," I said as I leaned over him.

He made a surprised sound as I pulled his underwear off and tossed it over my shoulder. He was definitely a natural blond. I let my nails lightly run over his cock and he shuddered. He was half-hard and I could already tell that he would be a bit over average size. I just hoped he knew how to use it.

I crawled up his body, letting my hair brush against his body as I went. I stayed on all fours above him as I leaned down and kissed him. I didn't make it gentle, forcing my tongue between his lips. I wanted him to know that he didn't have to worry about me breaking. I'd never been able to climax from sweet and slow alone. It always took something a little extra to get me over the edge.

When I broke the kiss, I slid back down his body until I was right where I wanted to be. I glanced up at him and then took him into my mouth. He groaned as I took his whole length. I knew that when he was at full size, I probably wouldn't be able to get it all in my mouth, and I didn't feel like showing up at work tomorrow with a sore throat.

His skin was hot and silky across my tongue and beneath my hand, that wonderful combination of hard and soft that nothing else could match. His hand rested on my head and I waited for him to take control, to push me down on his cock or maybe just dig his fingers into my hair. I'd been told more than once that I had wonderful hair to play with during sex. He didn't do either of those, merely kept his hand on my head as I moved up and down.

"Stop," he gasped. "I won't make it if you keep going."

I grinned and pushed myself up on my knees. He was fully erect now, but I wasn't going to fuck him. Not yet. If he was that close, he needed a bit of time to come down before we got to it.

"My turn," I said as I started to make my way back up his body.

He got onto his hands and knees. "Do you want your head on the pillows or flat?" He gestured towards the top of the bed.

I had to admit, I was a bit disappointed. Don't get me wrong, I wanted him to go down on me, but I'd wanted to be on top. I wanted to be able to control where his mouth went, how deep his tongue dipped. There were some guys that really knew how to please me with their mouth, but most of them needed either a map or me to take charge. I didn't let him see how I felt, though, as I stretched out on my back, letting my head rest at the base of the pillows so I could see him.

He lay down between my legs and lowered his head. I made an approving sound as he ran his tongue up the full length of me. When he slid it between my folds, I closed my eyes, wanting to just enjoy the sensation of friction and wet heat. I pictured Taylor's head between my thighs, his eyes peering up at me...

The picture shifted and I saw deep brown eyes, messy black hair. His face held the promise of something I'd never felt before...

Taylor's lips closed around my clit and I opened my eyes. Blond hair. Blue eyes. A focused determination as he swirled his tongue around that little bundle of nerves. Pleasure ran up my body and I cupped my breasts, teasing my nipples as Taylor continued to thoroughly lick me. It felt good, but there was none of the weight that promised an orgasm from oral alone. It wasn't that he was bad. He was actually pretty good, but my body just wasn't having it tonight.

"Condom?" I finally asked.

He looked up, surprised. "You're sure you're ready?"

I appreciated his concern, but I didn't think I was going to get anywhere without something bigger than a finger inside me. He was thick enough it was going to be tight, but more foreplay wasn't going to help that. Besides, sometimes it was better that way.

Taylor reached over to the nightstand and opened a drawer. He tore open a packet and rolled the latex over his cock. I watched with an almost detached disinterest. I had one hand on my breast, still playing with my nipple, and the other was between my legs, rubbing my clit as I waited.

When he leaned over me, I wrapped my hand around him and guided him inside. He groaned as he slid the first couple inches in.

"So fucking tight."

I put my hand around the back of his head and pulled it down towards my breast. It took him a moment, but he realized what I wanted and wrapped his lips around my nipple.

"Shit." I arched up against him as he started to suck. It was a straight line from my breast to my groin and as he continued to push into me, I started to feel that pressure that meant maybe I'd be able to get off after all.

He paused when he was completely inside me, lifting his head off of my breast. I could tell by the look on his face that he was fighting for control. I was suddenly tempted to squeeze him, see how far I could push him, but I didn't. If he came because I was teasing, he'd be embarrassed and I wouldn't be satisfied either. I liked him enough to not want to do that.

Finally, he propped himself up on his elbows and began to move. He had a nice, steady rhythm with long, sure strokes. He was big enough to make me feel full, but not so much that it hurt. His angle let him rub against my clit with just the right amount of pressure. I ran my hands up and down his back, lightly scratching my fingernails across the firm muscles of his ass. He made a sound in his throat when I did that and I smiled. He really was a great guy, and he did know what he was doing.

There was just one little problem. I was enjoying myself to an extent, and his movements felt good, but there was no edge, nothing that promised the release I needed. In fact, the only tension I could feel inside me was the lack of sex I'd experienced recently, and that would never work without some help.

When I was nineteen, I'd had a short-term relationship with a judo instructor and he'd taught me a couple self-defense moves that also worked well in the bedroom. I used one of them now to flip us over, putting Taylor underneath and me in control. His eyes were wide with surprise, but he didn't protest. Part of me wished he had. A nice little power struggle was always a turn-on.

His hands went to my hips, and I leaned forward, putting my palms flat on his chest. I rode him hard, trying to force my body to that place where I wouldn't have to think about being homesick, about living in a hotel...about my totally hot and untouchable boss.

DeVon wouldn't have laid passively beneath me, I was sure. I'd seen it in his eyes. He'd dig his fingers into my hips, leaving bruises. He'd fuck me hard enough to make me see stars. He wouldn't treat me like I could break, but he'd try to break me.

The thought of having DeVon pounding into me, his mouth and teeth marking me, his hands all over me, buried in my hair...

I came with a shudder, my body going stiff and clamping down on Taylor's cock. He cried out, his hips jerking up against me as he came. I slumped down on him, pressing my face against his chest to hide the guilt. Sure, I fantasized when I masturbated, but I didn't like to do it when I was with someone, especially someone I liked. Besides, Taylor was gorgeous. I shouldn't have needed...

I squeezed my eyes closed and pushed the thoughts out of my head. I rolled off of Taylor and he climbed out of bed to discard the condom. I turned my face away from him and gave in to the chemicals coursing through my body that told me to relax and sleep. I was half under when the bed dipped. I felt Taylor press his lips against my spine but didn't move. I didn't want him to know I was awake. He draped one arm across me and then I was asleep.

TWENTY-THREE

DEVON

Kelsee's painted red lips stretched wide around my cock as I fucked her mouth. She made a gagging sound as I pushed too far, but I held her there for a moment anyway, letting her struggle against the grip I had on her hair. She knew what to do if she wanted me to stop. She also knew that if she tapped out, she would get a taxi ride home, and that was it. She'd still be represented by Mirage, but she'd never get a second chance to fuck.

When I finally pulled her off my cock, she coughed and gasped for air. She definitely had a mouth made for oral, even if she did have to work on her gag reflex. I didn't give her a chance to recover as I pulled her to her feet. I'd already stripped her – not that it had been hard considering the only thing she'd been wearing under that thin dress had been skin – but I was still dressed. My pants weren't even down, just open.

I gave her a nudge towards the bed, releasing her hair. I slowly undressed as she climbed onto the large bed I'd bought just for nights like this. This was where I fucked, and this was where I sometimes let the women sleep if it was really late. I slept in my bedroom and always made sure I left a note with cab fare in it on the nightstand for them to find. In fact, the locked drawer in the top of the dresser had a stack of notes and twenties. The rest of the dresser was filled with other things, things that I was debating about using tonight.

My skin felt like it was on fire and every muscle in my body was tense. I needed release. Sometimes I liked to use the things I had in the dresser. Floggers and crops to discipline, nipple clamps and dildos of various sizes. Vibrators and butt plugs. Ropes, scarves, blindfolds, handcuffs and a spreader bar. I'd spent years collecting the best toys.

Tonight, I decided, I wanted to use my hands and my mouth. I just didn't know if I wanted her on her back or stomach first. It would all depend on how I planned on taking her, from behind or face-to-face. I made the choice almost immediately after I'd thought it. Behind. She was pretty, but I didn't want to see her face. This wasn't a personal connection. This was fucking.

"Lie on your back."

She did as she was told, spreading her legs before I said anything. That was fine. I intended to get there, just not yet. I stepped out of my underwear and walked over to the bed. I quickly cuffed Kelsee's hand to the headboard, then walked to the other side to do the same. I'd had the cuffs specially made. They were soft leather, the ones I used when I didn't want to leave marks where anyone could see them. They wouldn't hurt her, but she wouldn't be able to do anything, either. I left her legs free. She was too short for the restraints at the bottom of the bed unless I wanted to get the extensions, but I wasn't patient enough for that at the moment.

I climbed onto the bed, loving the way her eyes were so wide as they stared up at me. I kept my gaze on her face as I squeezed her breasts. She took a shuddering breath, but didn't make a sound. I rolled her nipples between my fingers and she moaned, arching her back. I pinched her hard and she whimpered. When I started to tug on her nipples, her mouth fell open. The harder I pulled, the harder she panted, until, finally, she cried out. Only then did I let her nipples go.

"I thought about putting clamps on those," I said as I moved to straddle her waist. "Making them so swollen and sore that you'll have to go topless all weekend." I leaned over and flicked my tongue across the tip of one nipple, then the other. Her body jerked with each touch.

"Yes," she said breathlessly. "Yes, please."

Without warning, I bit down on the nipple in front of me and she screamed, her entire body going rigid. Something deep inside me twisted as the errant thought popped into my head: would Krissy scream if I bit her? To clear my head, I turned to the other nipple and bit down, eliciting another scream. Before Kelsee could draw enough air for another cry, I took her nipple into my mouth and began to suck on it. This wasn't a gentle suckling to coax pleasure from a lover but a rough pull of my mouth, the kind that made the body beneath me writhe.

I ran my hand down over her flat stomach and slid my fingers between her legs. She'd closed them at some point when I'd been playing with her nipples, but I pushed them open. When I switched to the other breast, I shoved my middle finger into her pussy.

"Fuck!" Kelsee tugged on the restraints, but they didn't give. Stronger women than she had tested them.

I pumped my finger into her as I pulled at her breast with my lips, tongue and teeth. By the time I was done with them, her nipples were red and puffy, tender to even look at, and her entire body was shaking. She hadn't come yet, but I knew she was close. I withdrew my hand from between her legs and slid my finger between her lips. She didn't need me to tell her to suck.

"Don't come until I say you can," I said. "Understand?"

Kelsee nodded.

"If you disobey me," I added. "I'll fuck your ass dry." Her eyes widened but she didn't say anything.

I unsnapped the restraints and gave her a moment to rub the feeling back into her wrists as I repositioned them at the side of the bed.

"On your stomach."

She obeyed, but I saw her wince as her nipples touched the sheets. If she thought that hurt, she was going to be crying at the friction while I fucked her. I shrugged. She knew what she had to do if she wanted me to stop. If she didn't tap out, it was on her.

I stretched her arms out straight and tied them down again. I climbed onto the bed again and pulled her ankles together. I kept one hand on them as I ran my other hand over her ass. She didn't have much of one, not like...other women.

The first time my hand cracked against her ass, she yelped, her body jerking. A small sound of pain followed, but I had a feeling that was from her nipples. I'd practically been gentle. The second one was harder. I let her legs go as I alternated hands, my palms stinging as her ass turned from pink to red. She squirmed, trying to get away, but I'd done this too many times. I didn't miss a single stroke and I didn't stop until I knew anything more would bruise. If she'd been one of my girls, I would've kept going, and a part of me wanted to anyway.

I released her wrists and pulled her arms back. "Grab your ankles and pull your legs apart."

The position was impossibly awkward, but she did it, opening her legs wide enough for me to see that she was wet.

That was good, because I wasn't going to give her any foreplay. I picked up a condom from the nightstand and put it on. My cock was throbbing with everything that had built up from the moment I saw Krissy walk into my house with that asshole, Taylor.

I scowled as I positioned myself behind Kelsee. Was Krissy

going down on him? Did she come with his face buried in her pussy? Was he fucking her? Missionary? Doggie style?

The image of Krissy on all fours, her eyes glassy, mouth open, while Taylor slammed into her was too much.

I drove forward, burying myself in Kelsee's tight channel with one thrust. She wailed, almost losing her grip on her ankles. I grabbed her hair and yanked her head up. "If you let go, I'll use my crop on your tits, got it?"

She whimpered and tried to nod. I kept hold of her hair and used it as leverage. I didn't go slow; I didn't care if she'd adjusted to my size. I just wanted to fuck her hard enough that I forgot all about how Krissy was probably on her back, underneath Taylor.

I closed my eyes, forcing myself to think only of the body I was driving into, the way she squeezed around me, the sounds she made. No face. No name. Just curves and dips, hot and wet.

DeVon.

It was Krissy's voice in my ear, the low, husky way I imagined she'd say my name.

"Fuck!" I practically screamed it as I came. I ground my teeth together. This couldn't be happening again. I slammed my hand down on the bed and heard Kelsee squeak.

I opened my eyes. I'd forgotten about her. I was still inside her, and I'd forgotten about her.

And she hadn't come. Her entire body was tense and shaking. Her head was turned to the side enough that I could see the tears streaming down her face.

"Did you come?" My voice was rough as I asked the question.

She shook her head.

"You're allowed," I said. I put my hands beneath us, getting a finger slick with her juices. At the same time, I used my thumb to rub her clit while I pushed my finger into her ass.

She bent so far back as she came I thought her spine would snap. Her mouth was open, but no sound came out. All of her muscles went rigid, her pussy tightening around my cock hard enough to hurt, but it was the kind of pain that I needed right then and I shuddered.

Suddenly, she went limp, her limbs falling to the bed as she passed out. I pulled out of her and went to the guest bathroom to clean up enough to go to my own bedroom. Before I left, I pulled a blanket up over her and got one of my notes out of the dresser. I quietly shut the door behind me as I left and headed up to my own shower to wash away what I'd just done.

TWENTY-FOUR

KRISSY

When I first woke up, I couldn't figure out where I was. For a moment, I told myself it was because I was in a hotel instead of my own bed, but then I realized there was an arm around me and the memories of the night before flooded back to me.

Shit.

I eased myself out from underneath Taylor's arm and grabbed my dress from the floor. I dressed quickly, hoping the entire time that Taylor didn't wake up. I so didn't want to do the awkward morning after thing. I also wasn't going to do the whole leaving without a word thing. I found a pad of paper hanging on the refrigerator so I scribbled my number and said to call me.

I really did like Taylor, I thought as I hurried down the sidewalk to my car, but I remembered *everything* from the night before, including how DeVon had kept creeping up in my thoughts. I couldn't deny that I was attracted to DeVon, but I also could remind myself of all the shitty things he'd done to me. I did that the entire way back to the hotel and those thoughts followed me into sleep.

My phone ringing woke me hours later. I answered it with a groggy, "Hello?"

"Krissy? It's Taylor."

I sat up. "Oh, hey." Guess we were having the awkward morning after talk even though the clock said it was noon.

"So, I was wondering if you wanted to go out to dinner tonight." There was a pause, and then he added, "I had a great time last night."

"Me, too," I said. "I'd love to go to dinner."

"Great!"

She could almost hear that brilliant smile.

"Do you want me to pick you up?"

I hesitated. I wasn't sure I trusted myself to not invite him up if he drove me home tonight and I didn't know if I wanted two nights in a row. That felt a bit more like a commitment than I wanted. "Why don't we meet?"

"All right," he said amiably. "I'll text you the restaurant information."

"That sounds great."

I was glad he didn't linger on the phone. I had a lot to do today, not the least of which was picking out a dress for tonight and finding someone who could do something with my rat's nest of hair. I'd almost forgotten what a mess just-fucked hair could be. I really hoped it wasn't as bad when I had come in that morning as it felt now.

I also knew I had to start apartment hunting, but I could put that off until tomorrow. I'd worked my ass off this week. I deserved a little bit of fun. I kept telling myself that as I treated myself to a trip to the salon. By the time Taylor's text came in around four, I'd managed to get rid of all my previous guilt and was determined to make tonight perfect.

I arrived at the restaurant a few minutes after eight, but Taylor hadn't yet arrived. The host showed me to a secluded table in the back, then left me to admire the expensive white linen tablecloth and romantic candlelight. I was impressed. I knew Taylor didn't have much money. Getting a table like this in such a nice restaurant must've cost a fortune.

I took my phone out of my purse, figuring I might as well check my messages while I waited. That way, I'd be all caught up and could turn off my ringer, allowing Taylor and I to have an uninterrupted evening.

I had just finished replying to a text from Carrie telling me that she and Gavin were going to be planning a trip to LA soon when I caught movement across from me. I started to speak before I finished raising my head, "Hey, you're late..."

My voice trailed off but my mouth hung open as I saw that the man sitting across from me wasn't Taylor, but DeVon. I snapped my jaw shut, my brain scrambling for a moment before righting itself.

"What are you doing here?" I was aware that sounded rude, but to be fair, he was the one who'd just sat down, uninvited. I sat up straighter. I didn't have any reason to be polite. We weren't at work or a business dinner or anything like that. This was my personal time. "You have to go," I said firmly. "I'm on a date."

DeVon gave me an annoying smirk that made me want to slap him. I clenched my hands together on my lap to resist the impulse.

"I'm sorry, Krissy. I know I shouldn't intrude, but I thought you might like to know that Taylor won't be coming."

"What?" I couldn't have heard him correctly. How the hell did he know who I was meeting? And why was it any of his business?

"He knows the rule about no dating between clients and agents."

I frowned at him. Was he seriously going to pull that bullshit again? "He's not a Mirage client."

DeVon's smirk widened. "He is now. I just signed him."

TWENTY-FIVE

KRISSY

DeVon fucking Ricci. I ground my teeth together and pushed the gas pedal closer to the floor. He'd gotten the upper hand again, and used my personal life to do it. Why the hell was he so interested in who I was dating? Control freak. At least it wasn't like I'd been in love with Taylor or anything. He'd been fun, a distraction like all the men I'd been with in New York had been. And I knew I was the same for him. After all, he never would've signed with Mirage if he'd been looking for something serious. Like DeVon had said, Taylor knew the rules about not dating clients.

If Taylor had come himself and said Mirage was going to sign him, I wouldn't have even been mad. I would've been happy for him. The fact that DeVon had felt like he needed to come tell me himself only proved what a sadistic prick he was.

A flash of red and blue in my rearview mirror caught my eye a second before I heard the brief wail of a siren.

Fuck.

Could this day get any worse? I thought as I pulled over. I got my license out as well as the car's registration. I really hoped I wasn't going to get in trouble at work because I'd gotten pulled over in the company car.

"Good evening, Miss."

I looked up to see a handsome face looking down at me. He had dark hair and eyes, but any resemblance to DeVon stopped there. That was good. The cop was good-looking in a different way. Not that it made any difference as he told me how fast I'd been going and wrote out a citation. I was polite and smiled at him, but what I really wanted to do was curse. Not at him. It wasn't his fault I'd been speeding. No, that blame belonged to someone else.

DeVon fucking Ricci.

I made it back to the hotel without further incident and dropped into bed without bothering to change. I just wanted to sleep and forget about the entire day.

The problem was, every time I closed my eyes, all I kept seeing was DeVon. Those wild dark waves and deep brown eyes. His strong jawline and firm chest. Those broad shoulders and kissable lips.

"Fuck!" I shouted into my pillow.

Why, of all the people in the world, did I have to keep thinking about my asshole of a boss? Sure, he'd made an impression, but I hadn't thought it was a good one. Then, last night, while Taylor had been going down on me, I'd had a flash of DeVon between my legs. It had been DeVon I'd pictured beneath me while I'd been riding Taylor, and it had been the thought of him that had made me come.

I sighed and rolled over onto my back. Did he feel the same way about me? Was that the real reason he'd signed Taylor? Because he liked me? I shook my head, almost laughing at the idea. DeVon wasn't like that. He was just playing games. That's the kind of person he was, after all. The kind of man who'd show up in a hotel room with two naked women and make an offer of an orgy just to test to see if I'd do it. That kind of man always made sure he was in control. He made the rules of the game but none of those rules seemed to apply to him. What a hypocrite.

I squeezed my eyes closed. What was I doing here? Why had I even taken this job? Had I made a mistake?

"No." I said it out loud.

I'd come to Hollywood to make a career for myself. A career that I wanted and deserved. I hadn't let my mother guilt me into going home and I wasn't going to let anyone else stand in my way. I was a grown woman, strong and confident. I'd made my way without anyone's help and I could do this. I wasn't going to let DeVon take me down.

I slowly exhaled, letting all of the negative energy out with the air. My mom's sixth girlfriend, Felicity, had been a yoga instructor. Most of my sophomore year of high school had been spent in the lotus position.

I let my mind go blank and waited to fall asleep.

TWENTY-SIX

DEVON

My hand was aching as I set down the receiver, and my joints protested as I let go. I was actually surprised that I hadn't managed to crack the plastic while I'd yelled at the number one casting agent for Universal Studios.

"What the fuck is wrong with me?" I muttered as I leaned back in my chair. My entire body was tense, my heart racing. Sure, the guy hadn't exactly been polite, but I'd never lost my temper with him before. No one yelled at Theodore Kahn, not if they wanted to stay in the business.

Fuck. I ran my hand through my hair and tried to regain my composure. I had to fix this before it got out of hand.

I reached for the phone again. In this business, you didn't say an apology with a phone call, you said it with something sickeningly expensive. My assistant was out running errands. I'd just add another to her list and it'd be taken care of.

I didn't bother with a greeting. "Send a bottle of Glenfiddich single malt whisky to the casting agent for Universal, Theodore Kahn."

She didn't ask why or even sound surprised as she told me she'd take care of it. I made a mental note to make sure she got a bigger Christmas bonus this year.

After I put down the phone, I leaned forward, placing my elbows on my desk and pressing my fingertips together. I really needed to pull my shit together. This wasn't like me at all. I was always in control. I lived it. Breathed it. I had control over my life, over my business, my finances, my employees, my women. But for the last couple days, I'd been off balance. I'd lost control twice while fucking, once even coming before my partner. Unless a punishment was being given, I always made sure my sub came first. But I hadn't been able to stop myself, and it ate at me. Being able to control myself was part of who I was, and I was losing it.

The bigger problem was that I knew why.

Krissy fucking Jensen.

I was always thinking about her. I'd been picturing her with her mouth stretched around my cock when I'd lost control that first time. Then, when I'd been with Kelsee, I'd been seeing and hearing Krissy. And it wasn't just during sex. She'd pop into my mind at the worst moments, making me lose my train of thought.

Why'd I hire her? I shook my head. I knew why. I wanted to fuck her and dump her, just like the others.

But I couldn't.

I'd been right when I'd said she was talented and would be a huge asset to Mirage. She was shaping up to be the most promising new agent I'd signed in a long time – hell, basically in forever. She was too valuable for me to fuck and dump.

I felt a familiar pain in my heart telling me that I was lying to myself and I scowled. No. I wasn't going to go there. It was always painful, and never resolved anything.

I needed something to get me out of my own head, something that promised a release of all this tension. I opened the top drawer to my right and pulled out a little black book. I started to flip through the pages, skimming over the names.

Eliza. Maryann. Tisha. Kendra. Roni. Angelica.

"That's the one," I muttered as I picked up my cell phone. These kinds of calls didn't go on the company phone. I dialed the number.

"Hello?" Her voice was sugary sweet.

"Angelica, I want to fuck tonight." One of the things I liked about her was I didn't need to try to seduce her.

She chuckled, a low, throaty sound that promised all sorts of decadent things.

"Is that so?" she asked. "Are you hard for me?"

"Depends." I gave her the usual answer. "Are you wet for me?"

"Babe, I'm always wet for you," she said with a purr.

"Such a little slut," I said. "Make sure you're completely prepared. It's going to be a long night."

"Promise?"

I hung up without answering, knowing that she'd spend the rest of the day making sure everything was perfect when I arrived, her entire body ready for me to use it however I wanted.

I adjusted my tie and smiled. I was feeling better already, and I had something enjoyable to look forward to tonight. The day was looking up.

TWENTY-SEVEN

KRISSY

JASON reaches for LISA and they kiss. It's hard and hungry, bruising. This is one of those "we're all going to die" kisses. The clothes come off, tearing and ripping. It's almost frantic, like they're afraid if they don't hurry, they'll die before they get to the good stuff.

A tapping sound interrupted the visual I was working on for the screenplay I was reading. I sighed as I looked up. The story was really good, and I was hoping to get at least one of my two clients to read for it. In fact, I could almost see Taylor playing the lead, Jason, and was debating if I wanted to find out who was representing Taylor to suggest it.

Tracy was tapping her pencil on the glass wall that separated us. When she saw that she had my attention, she gestured to the right. Movement caught my eye, but I couldn't see well enough to tell exactly what was going on. I put the screenplay down and stood. Men, dressed in matching work clothes with a company logo, were moving furniture out of an office. It was George Hamilton's office.

I hadn't reported him to HR for what he'd said my first day

here, or even spoken about it, but I knew the gossip had made the rounds. Very little was kept secret in a place like this. I just didn't know how many people were on my side versus his.

I opened the door. "What's going on?" I asked Tracy.

"I don't know," she answered. "It looks like Mr. Hamilton is being relocated."

I gave her a look. "Relocated, my ass. That looks more like an 'escorting out of here' move."

Tracy grinned, and I was just about to smile back when I saw George storming towards me, his face beet red, hands clenched into fists.

"And here he comes," I said as I went back into my office and took a seat behind my desk again. I wanted something between us if this went down like I thought it was going to.

George didn't even pause by Tracy's desk. He threw open my door and stormed over to my desk. He put his fists on it and leaned across. "You did this, you fucking whore."

I stood up because I didn't like him looking down at me. At least with my heels I was closer to his height. "I have no idea what you're talking about," I said in my most sugar-sweet voice. "But I'll be happy to tell HR how welcoming you were when I first got here, if you think that'll help."

"You fucking *bitch*." He practically spat the words at me before spinning around and walking out of my office. As the door started to close behind him, I saw something fall from one of the boxes. I couldn't see too clearly, but it looked like some sort of baseball collector's item.

"You fucking assholes! Watch what you're doing or I'll sue you for more than you make in a year. Your grandkids' grandkids will be paying it off!"

As George stalked away, I glanced at Tracy, who grinned at me. When she turned her attention back to her computer, I put my elbows on the desk and rested my face in my hands. I let out a breath. I was a lawyer, so I liked to argue, but I didn't like confrontations like that.

This was so fucked up. Was George right? Had word of what had happened between us gotten back to DeVon?

I stood up. I needed to find out what was going on. I didn't look at Tracy as I walked out of my office and headed towards the elevator. My annoyance grew on the short ride and by the time the doors opened, I was tapping my fingers against my leg. DeVon's secretary said something as I walked past, but I ignored her.

DeVon looked up as I barged in, a flash of surprise going across his eyes. I didn't give him a chance to speak.

"Why the fuck did you fire George?"

A smile spread across DeVon's face and he leaned back in his chair, folding his hands in front of him.

He didn't answer my question, so I continued, "Is this another one of your fucking tests? Is George some actor you hired to insult me just so you could fire him and make yourself look like less of an asshole?" I had a moment to wonder if someday I'd go too far and he'd fire me, but I pushed the thought aside, letting my temper continue to carry me. "Was that your plan all along? What's the—"

"Stop."

The word was quiet, but it did what DeVon wanted. My mouth snapped shut.

"I have a perfectly good reason to fire George. You might not have known this, but he's been a pretty naughty boy."

I scowled. "No surprise there. I know a few naughty boys around here."

DeVon chuckled, and I tried to ignore the way that sound made heat bloom in my stomach.

"Last year, we had a sexual harassment suit against George brought against us by his former assistant. It cost us a hundred and fifty thousand to fight it. But, he was acquitted, so I didn't fire him...then. However, it looks like he's been up to his old tricks again. I don't care to finance another lawsuit, particularly if he's guilty, so I fired him. Does that answer your question?"

My anger had boiled down, but I still wasn't sure I believed what DeVon was saying. "Yeah, I suppose so...except why did he say *I* was the cause if all this was because he was harassing his assistant?"

"I never said he was harassing Amanda," DeVon said mildly. "Now, don't you have work to attend to?" He leaned forward and buzzed his secretary. "Get me Pete Marrow on the phone."

He looked up at me, and I realized I was standing there with my mouth hanging open like an idiot.

"Was there anything else?"

Heat flooded my face. "No." I left, giving DeVon's secretary an apologetic smile that she didn't appear to care for. My head was spinning as I got on the elevator.

I didn't understand DeVon at all. Had Hamilton been right? Had the story about our encounter on my first day made it up to DeVon and he'd fired George because of it? I didn't have any proof, but I knew it was the truth. DeVon also would've known that I hadn't gone to HR about it. The fact that he'd still fired George meant it was about more than wanting to avoid legal action. It meant that I meant something to him. What that was, I wasn't sure, and I didn't know if DeVon's actions meant I should feel flattered or horrified. Both were legitimate options.

TWENTY-EIGHT

DEVON

I tightened my grip on her thick, dark hair, but instead of pulling her head back, I pushed her face forward into the couch cushion. Her scream was muffled as another orgasm ripped through her. I didn't even slow down as I pounded into her ass. We'd been fucking for over an hour, and I was almost at the end. The belt I'd used on her back and ass was now wrapped around her wrists. Her skin was red and hot under my hand, and I dug my fingers into her hip. She moaned and writhed, pushing back to meet my thrusts.

I'd been right. Angelica had been exactly what I'd needed to take out my frustration. Dark hair and eyes, curves, and a penchant for pain. She'd come twice just from the belt, and then again when I'd gone down on her. I lost count after I'd started fucking her, but I knew it was a lot. She always came a lot, but tonight she was screaming louder than usual, which I took to be a positive sign.

I reached between her legs and shoved the dildo deeper into her pussy and she wailed, her bound hands thumping against the cushion above her head. Her ass tightened around me as she came again, and that was it. I groaned as I slammed into her, driving her off her fuck-me heels as spots exploded behind my eyes. I stayed there for only a moment, letting go of her hair and pulling out of her ass so fast that her entire body shuddered. I heard her gasp in air as she raised her head. The gasp turned into a wordless cry when I yanked out the dildo, leaving her completely empty for the first time since I'd arrived.

I disposed of the condom while she rolled herself onto the couch. She held up her bound hands and I raised an eyebrow. She dropped to her knees in front of me and opened her mouth. Briefly, I considered seeing if she could get me hard again, but it was getting late. I leaned down, grabbed her jaw and kissed her, forcing my tongue deep inside her mouth. Only when I was satisfied did I straighten, and then untied her hands.

I looked around for my clothes as she flopped back down onto the couch.

"Wow," she said. "That was fucking amazing. What drugs did you take tonight?"

"Drugs?" I scowled at her and tried not to think about how I'd been picturing doing all of this to Krissy. "What the fuck? You think I can't do that without drugs?" I snapped my belt. "Do I need to correct you?"

She spread her legs. She was so wet that we both knew how much the leather would hurt, but we also knew how much she loved it. Instead of giving me a standard response, however, she pulled a cigarette from a nearby pack and lit it. "That sounds like fun, but my husband's gonna be home in like thirty minutes. You better take off."

I bristled at the near command. Someone was forgetting her place. Still naked, I walked over to her and took the cigarette from between her lips. I stubbed it out on an ashtray as I put my knee on the couch, right between her legs. I yanked her head back with one hand so that she was looking up at me. The other hand went to the platinum stud in her nipple. I twisted it and she whimpered, arching her back to push her breast into my hand.

"Listen to me," I hissed. My usually faint accent thickened. "I'm in charge, and if I want to stay and fuck you until dawn, that's what I'm going to do." I ground my knee against her and she moaned. "And if that means your husband walks in and sees what an unfaithful little slut he's married to, then so be it."

I tugged on her piercing and felt her body start to shake. Her hips started to move against my leg as she looked for another climax. I released her and took a step back. Someone was forgetting our agreement, which meant it was time to remind her.

I picked up my clothes and started to get dressed. When I glanced up at her, she had a hand between her legs, rubbing her clit, and sliding her fingers in and out of her pussy. I kept my expression disinterested and pulled on my shirt as if that held far more interest for me than her body. Ignoring her was far worse than any insult I could come up with.

I was halfway to the door when she spoke.

"When will I see you again?"

I reached for the doorknob and didn't even bother to look at her when I answered, "Write me a Christmas card. Maybe I'll reply in July."

I didn't even try to hide my self-satisfied grin as I climbed into my car. All of that pent-up frustration and tension had just ended in one of my best nights. I'd played Angelica like an instrument, every orgasm telling me what I already knew. I'd been good tonight.

Fuck that. I'd been *great*.

Things were always better when I did them my way. Everyone got what they deserved, and no one could touch me.

People getting what they deserved turned my thoughts towards my encounter with Krissy earlier that day. I had to admit, I'd enjoyed her coming into my office and questioning me about firing George. Her face had been flushed, her eyes flashing, and I'd wondered what it would take to tame her.

Not that I was going to. She was off limits to be brought under submission, but just because I wasn't going to fuck her didn't mean I couldn't fuck *with* her.

I chuckled. Krissy all but accused me of firing George just to get in good with her, but the truth was, he'd had the worst conversion rate of all my agents. Keeping him at a hundred, twenty-five thousand a year plus bonuses – not that he'd really ever made any – hadn't been prudent. The incident with Krissy had just been a good excuse.

A flare of anger went through me when I thought about what I'd overheard two people saying had happened between George and Krissy. I told myself it was because a part of me wished it was true, that Krissy really had slept with me to get the job. Not because she didn't deserve the job otherwise, but because at least then I'd have gotten it out of my system and wouldn't have had such a shit week.

Images flashed through my mind. They were all from what I'd done tonight, but in each one, it was Krissy, not Angelica. Krissy's mouth I was fucking. Her ass gripping my cock. Her skin reddening as she begged for more.

My cock twitched.

"Fuck," I muttered. I was getting hard again and I didn't want to go to bed with a hard-on...again. And I certainly didn't want to take care of it myself. Aside from the fact that I didn't need to, I knew that Krissy would play a leading role in any masturbatory fantasy I came up with. I wanted to *stop* thinking about her, not fantasize about her.

Who could I call?

I glanced up at a neon sign for Chinese food. That sounded good. Mika was nothing like Krissy. For some reason, Mika's number wasn't in my phone, so I recited it from memory, then waited for my Bluetooth to connect me.

"Hello?" A young woman answered.

"I would like my little Chinese special," I said.

"Chinese special?" The woman sounded confused.

She must've been new, I thought. "Yeah, my usual. This is DeVon." That should've been enough.

"Oh, I'm sorry, Mr. DeVon. This isn't a Chinese restaurant. You've reached–"

Was she kidding me? "I know this isn't a Chinese restaurant!" I was almost yelling. I wasn't in the mood to be screwed with. "Just put Mika on the phone. She's my little Chinese special."

The woman's voice turned cold and hard. "You have the wrong number, Mr. DeVon. This is not a restaurant or a bordello. This is Sister Mary Margaret of Our Lady of the Sacred Heart. You can call any time you need prayer or counseling, but for other...services, I would ask that you refrain from calling back."

Heat flooded my face as I slammed my finger into the Bluetooth button on my steering wheel. I pressed the accelerator to the floor and sped past two old women in a rusted Chevy Impala. Great fucking way to end the night.

TWENTY-NINE

KRISSY

"You're kidding me," Carrie said incredulously. "He didn't do that."

I nodded. "He did. He fired the guy on account of me. George insulted me and that's what happened."

George had actually been fired two days ago, but since I'd gotten a call from Carrie saying she was coming in this weekend, I hadn't bothered to tell her any of this over the phone. Aside from the fact that I'd wanted to save it for a face-to-face conversation, I'd also gotten another call right in the middle of her telling me her plans. Carrie's trip to LA turned out to be perfect timing. I'd gotten one of the apartments I'd applied for, which meant she would arrive just in time to help me move in to my new place. After a busy morning and afternoon emptying the moving van I'd had in a paid lot since it'd arrived, everything was at least in my new, two-bedroom West Hollywood apartment, though not much of it was unpacked. It was nearly seven by the time Carrie and I finally sat down for a well-deserved meal. That was when I'd spilled the whole story.

Carrie shook her head. "Unless you'd reported him for sexual harassment, which you didn't, that's not a legitimate reason to fire him." She grinned at me. "Sorry, not that you're not special."

I rolled my eyes and tried not to let Carrie see how much I'd missed this, sitting down and talking to her. "Well, he said it was also because of some previous lawsuit." I put down my near-empty glass. "Fuck it. I'm tired of talking about DeVon and my job. Come on." I stood. "Let's go out and see what the Hollywood nightlife has to offer in this part of the city."

I managed to find one of my favorite dresses, the kind that looked painted on and was guaranteed to get me laid. Carrie had brought clubbing clothes, and while she'd definitely loosened up since she'd started dating Gavin, there was almost twice as much fabric to her outfit as there was to mine. Still, I had to admit that she looked hot. Being in love agreed with her.

All eyes were on us as we made our way through one of Hollywood's hottest clubs. We weren't famous, but we were gorgeous, and running Club Privé had certainly taught Carrie how to work a room. We were on our third round of drinks when I decided I wanted to dance. Carrie excused herself to the restroom, and I made my way onto the dance floor.

An arm slid around my waist, turning me around so that I was looking directly at the very muscular chest of one of the hottest guys I'd seen so far since I'd arrived in this town. Thick dark hair and eyes, both of which could've been brown or black. His shirt was fitted and his pants rode that line of being too tight, but both showed off his considerable assets. He looked younger than me, but he'd gotten in, so I was counting on him being at least twenty-one.

We didn't speak as we danced together, grinding our bodies against each other until I could feel how hard he was. He pulled me closer, his hands on my ass, and leaned down so that he could speak in my ear.

"You know where you want to go tonight."

I raised an eyebrow. "Oh, I do?"

"Yeah," he said with a cocky grin. "Home with me."

I laughed. He actually thought he'd get to be in charge. How cute. "I was actually hoping *you'd* come home with *me*."

"Krissy." A hand on my arm reminded me that I hadn't come alone.

The guy's eyes lit up as his gaze raked over Carrie. "Oh, a threesome. I can get into that."

Carrie rolled her eyes. "Keep dreaming, hot stuff. I'm just going to steal my friend for a second here."

I let her pull me away from the dance floor and felt the guy's eyes on me. I put a little extra sway into my hips. I was pleasantly buzzed and enjoying myself. I'd almost forgotten how much I loved going out with friends.

"I hate to spoil the party," Carrie said. "But I'm exhausted. Jet lag."

Instantly, I felt like a shitty friend. She was still on East Coast time and it was – I glanced at my watch – almost five in New York.

I nodded. "Give me a minute." I walked back onto the dance floor and cut between the guy I'd been dancing with and a girl who'd tried to take my spot. I ignored the girl's protest and stuck my hand in the guy's pocket. His eyes widened as I fished around more than necessary before I pulled out his phone. I dialed my number from his phone, then handed it back to him.

"I'll call you," I said as I sauntered away, confident that his eyes were glued to my ass. As I went to save his number, I realized that I didn't know his name. I shrugged. That wasn't really a problem. I didn't usually scream a guy's name when we fucked, and I wasn't taking him home to meet the family. I saved the number under 'Club Hottie' and put my phone back into my purse.

Carrie grinned at me as we left the club, but I waited until we were out in the comparative silence before I asked her what she thought was so funny.

"You," she said. "New city, new time zone, same Krissy." She linked her arm through mine as we started to walk towards my apartment. "I'd been worried that moving here might change you."

I grimaced as my heels pinched my feet. Another way LA and New York were different: cabs. Back East, there were always cabs around the clubs, ready to take home inebriated partiers. Here, half the time, they were few and far between. I paused and pulled off my heels. That, at least, was a positive. I could walk in my bare feet at two in the morning during the first weeks of autumn and my feet weren't even chilly.

"I'm going to miss you," I said suddenly. "I mean, I was already missing you, but now that you've been here, when you leave, it's going to be so much worse."

Carrie squeezed my arm. "I've missed you, too, but I promise that I'll keep coming to visit as often as I can."

"Definitely a perk of being your own boss," I said. "Or sleeping with the boss."

Carrie rolled her eyes. "Gavin's not my boss." She gave me a mischievous look. "And I'm not the one whose *boss* wants her."

I shook my head. "DeVon doesn't want me. He just likes fucking with people."

Carrie didn't argue, but I could see on her face that she didn't agree with me. Instead, she flagged down the only cab we'd seen so far. The ride back to my apartment was quiet, but it wasn't a bad kind of quiet. For the first time since I'd moved out here, I felt comfortable. When we got back to my new place, we both kicked off our shoes and headed for my bedroom. The only things that were set up were my bed, a small kitchen table with two matching chairs and a love seat that was full of boxes. It didn't really look like home, but with Carrie there, it kinda felt like it.

We dropped onto the bare mattress. I didn't even know where my sheets or blankets were, but it was warm enough that it didn't matter. Carrie rolled onto her side, but I stayed on my back, staring up at the ceiling. I'd missed this. My old life had been so uncomplicated. Go to work. Go out with friends. Hook up with guys. Repeat.

"I think I should come home." It was the first time I'd actually spoken the words out loud. I felt the bed dip as she turned to face me, but I didn't look at her. "I mean, Mimi would give me my old job back, or I could just find another one."

"Even though I would love to have you back in New York, I don't think you should give up." Carrie's voice was soft. "You really wanted this. Paradise compared to boring divorce law. And I know you love it here, no matter how tough it can be."

She was right, and I knew it.

"Just give yourself some time. You're going to be homesick."

"I wasn't when I moved from Chicago to New York," I countered.

"You wanted out of Chicago," she reminded me. "And you have family in New York."

She was right, again. Technically, my biological family was in Chicago, but my *real* family was Carrie and Leslie and Dena. I didn't have anyone like that here. I was a people person, always had been, and there wasn't anyone in LA worth staying for.

The image of DeVon popped into my head, and I tried to push it away. I just needed time, and I'd make friends, meet new people. This place could become home. I tried to hold onto that thought until I fell asleep, but DeVon kept forcing his way back in. Finally, I gave up and let myself think about him until I finally went under.

THIRTY

KRISSY

It was harder not to cry when I dropped Carrie off at LAX than I'd thought it'd be. Tears were burning my eyes but I kept reminding myself of a trick my drama teacher had taught me when it came to controlling my emotions, and I managed to keep them back. As I watched her walk away, I was struck with the nearly overwhelming desire to buy a ticket and board with her, leave all of this behind and go home.

New York wasn't home, I told myself firmly. Not anymore. I had to stop thinking that way if I was going to give LA a fair shot. And Carrie had been right. I needed to give this a chance. It had been challenging, but nothing I hadn't been able to handle. Just because something was tough didn't mean I should give up. If I gave up and returned to New York just because it was hard, I'd never forgive myself. My parents would use it as justification for their belief that I couldn't hack it on my own. No. My resolve solidified. Sure, there were some things about LA that I didn't like, but I'd also already gotten to experience things that I never could've in New York.

And then there was DeVon. I sighed as I watched Carrie go through security. There was something about him. The more I thought about it, the more sure I was that he had feelings for me. He was trying to play off the whole George thing as business, but I didn't think that was the case. I was sure he'd heard about what George had said, and that was why he'd fired him.

Not that it mattered, I reminded myself. He was smoldering hot and sexy as hell, but I couldn't imagine myself with him. I ignored the voice in the back of my head that reminded me I had, in fact, imagined myself with him. At least in bed with him. I was sure he'd be amazing, but I didn't want to dwell on it. Those had been flukes, I told myself. DeVon was a womanizer. Then again, I was a self-proclaimed man-eater, so I supposed we were on equal footing there.

There was a difference, though. In the past, even when I'd dated players, I'd been in charge. They all knew going into it that I wasn't interested in commitment, and I was always the one calling the shots. I decided how far things went and when they ended. With DeVon, I knew that things would be different. I couldn't imagine him letting anyone kick him to the curb. He'd made it clear that everything happened on his terms, and I was sure that carried over to his personal life. What if I wanted more than one night? Not a relationship, of course, but what if I wanted us to be fuck buddies like some of the guys I'd been friends with back in New York, but he didn't want it? What if we fucked once and that was it because that was all he wanted, to prove that he could have whatever he wanted, including me? As much as I hated to think it, that might actually hurt, and I'd promised myself I'd never let a man hurt me again. Pete had done enough damage.

I pushed the thoughts of my asshole ex from my mind as I waved a last goodbye to Carrie, then headed to the parking lot. My red Beamer was waiting. It was similar to the ones Mirage had, but this one was mine. Granted, it was a lease and not an outright buy, but at least I didn't have to use any of my parents' money for it.

I let myself think about nothing but the pleasure of driving my car as I headed back to my apartment. I loved the neighborhood, the building and the apartment itself, but it was hard not to feel the emptiness when I went inside. I hadn't been here alone yet and I didn't like the feeling. I'd spent my first weekends here trying to get things together and going to parties with Taylor, but now I didn't have any plans. Back in New York, I never spent weekends alone. I always had company, even if it was just one of the girls and me watching marathons of scary movies while eating popcorn. If I had a guy over instead of a girl, there'd be making out and maybe more. Either way, it was never just me.

I sighed and started unpacking. At least I could get some of that done since my best friend was gone and the only guy I sort of liked was now off-limits because my sadistic and narcissistic employer had made absolutely certain that we couldn't have anything together by offering Taylor the one thing he wanted more than me. A contract with Mirage.

By the time I showered and crawled into bed – this time with sheets – I was emotionally exhausted and ready to lose myself in sleep. Just before I drifted off, my phone dinged. I groaned and looked over at it.

It was a text from DeVon.

Why would he be texting me so late on a weekend? A thrill of excitement went through me. Maybe I'd gotten my first read for one of my clients. I opened the text and had to read it twice to make sure I was reading it correctly.

"What are you wearing?"

Was he fucking *kidding* me?

THIRTY-ONE

DEVON

I was only half-listening as my buddy Sandy talked about us heading to Vegas and hooking up with some strippers this weekend.

"Remember that time you called three strippers and..."

My door slammed open, and I lost the rest of whatever story Sandy was starting to tell as Krissy stormed in. Damn, she was sexy when she was pissed.

"What the fuck is wrong with you? Do you want me to file a sexual harassment suit or what?"

I didn't take my eyes off of her as I spoke into the phone. "I'll have to call you back." I hung up before Sandy could say anything, then leaned back in my chair and waited to see what happened next. Krissy was one of the only people whose actions I couldn't always predict.

"Are you even listening to me?" she snapped.

I raised an eyebrow and tried not to leer at her. There was color high on her cheeks and her eyes were almost black. She was also breathing hard, which meant those amazing breasts of hers were heaving and it was all I could do not to look at them. Instead, I played the obvious card.

"Do I have to remind you who you're talking to right now? I am your boss, not your boyfriend."

She moved a step closer to my desk. "You sent me a text last night asking me what I was wearing. I repeat, what the hell is wrong with you?"

Both eyebrows went up this time and I put on my best expression of innocent surprise, though I was neither surprised nor innocent.

"Oh, was that what I wrote? I was wondering why you didn't reply. I intended to ask 'what are you wearing *tomorrow*?' Referring, of course, to *today* since we have an important lunch meeting with Jake Morris." I kept my voice even, partly because she did need to know this, but also because I got the feeling it made her angrier when I stayed calm, and that amused me. "You remember Jake, the casting direction from Universal? Now is your time to shine." I stood up and gave her a once over. "We need to present sexy Krissy. And this is exactly why I texted last night. You can't wear that." I pointed at the drab dress she was wearing. "It's boring." I didn't add that she could make a potato sack sexy. That wasn't the point.

"Is that why you hired me?" Her temper was still going. "So you can show me off to your golf buddies, and have me be the price for a contract?"

A muscle in my jaw twitched and I could feel my calm dissolving. "Don't pretend to be such a saint. It's not like you didn't realize what was going to happen, like you weren't warned. I told you that Hollywood thrives on tits and ass. I don't make you whore yourself out, but flaunting what you have—*that*, you knew, was part of the deal."

She sighed, but it wasn't an 'I give up' sigh, rather more of a 'why do I bother with you' sound. "What does it matter anyway?

It's not like I didn't already know you're a dickhead and a fucking hedonist."

I frowned. "You know, Krissy, English isn't my first language. I don't like it when I have to look up words in the dictionary." Sarcasm dripped from my words.

She uttered a short laugh. "I could leave right now."

Something twisted in my stomach.

"I don't need this job," she continued. "I could just walk right out of here and take the next plane back to New York. I–"

I slammed my hands down on my desk to get her to stop saying things I didn't want to hear. "You wouldn't walk out of here." My accent was back, but I didn't even try to get it under control. I stepped around my desk. "You wouldn't, because..." I cut the distance between us to less than a foot. I growled the rest of the sentence, "You are just like me!"

Suddenly, her hands were fisting in my shirt, and she was yanking me towards her, her mouth rising to meet mine. I had only a second to be surprised and then she was kissing me.

THIRTY-TWO

KRISSY

I didn't know what came over me. I was just so angry, and everything just sort of happened. I didn't even give myself a moment to second-guess what I was doing. Instead, I tilted my head and opened my mouth, pushing my tongue between his lips. He made a sound that went straight south, and his arms wrapped around me, crushing me against his chest. Our mouths battled for dominance, tongues twisting as they fought, teeth scraping and biting until the heat inside me was nearly unbearable. I knew he felt it, too. His cock was hardening against my stomach, and my pussy throbbed.

I pulled back, needing the air for my head as much as my lungs. I shook my head. "We can't do this." I was practically gasping. "What about the rules?" It was a stupid excuse, I knew, but it was all I had at the moment.

"Fuck the rules." His voice was low and dark. "They're there to be broken."

He pulled me towards him, lowering his mouth to mine before my hormone-altered brain could formulate any sort of response. I expected more bruising force, a show to remind me who was in charge, but that wasn't what happened. Instead, his lips moved with mine as he slowly explored my mouth. It wasn't gentle or sweet, but firm in a different kind of way. This was the sort of kiss that promised wonderful things. A kiss that started a fire only he could quench. A promise of all the decadent things he could do to my body while I begged him to never stop.

I was almost trembling as his hands slid down my back to my ass, and one started to pull up my skirt. I tensed and the hands that were clutching his shirt now pushed back on that oh-so-firm chest. I wasn't going to do this.

"I-I have to go change for the meeting." I barely managed to get the words out. I smoothed down my skirt as I hurried out of the office on legs that almost couldn't hold me. I knew my face was flushed, and I really hoped that anyone who saw me would just think I was still angry.

My head was still spinning as I drove home. What the fuck had just happened? Had I lost my mind, kissing DeVon? And then letting him kiss me a second time?

"Dammit." I smacked my hand on the steering wheel. Why hadn't I gone back to New York with Carrie?

I managed to pull myself together by the time I returned to the office in a different outfit. If anyone thought it was strange that I'd come in wearing something stylish but plain, then left and returned in something quite a bit more form-fitting, they didn't say it. I supposed what DeVon said was true. Tits and ass. Everyone knew how it worked here.

I stayed in my office the rest of the morning, buried in a screen-play I wasn't really reading. I kept waiting for DeVon to come down and say that we needed to talk, but he didn't come. Then I started wondering if he was just going to wait until I closed his deal with Jake and then fire me. When it was time to leave for the lunch, my stomach was in knots, and I didn't think I'd be able to eat a bite.

I arrived first and was shown to the table. I'd only been there for a few minutes when DeVon showed up. I automatically tensed, but he just gave me a once over like he'd done earlier, except this time he nodded in approval. I followed his lead in not talking about what had happened, figuring he didn't want Jake to arrive in the middle of what was already going to be an awkward conversation. He ordered wine for the table, then asked about an appetizer. I answered politely, though I doubted I'd even be able to swallow anything.

Just as the waiter was returning with our drinks, DeVon's phone buzzed. He glanced down at it, then set it aside.

"Jake had to cancel." He took a sip of the wine and nodded to the waiter. "Since we're here, we might as well eat." Without asking what I wanted, he ordered for us both.

I would've been annoyed if I hadn't been so nervous. If he hadn't been my boss, this would've been so much easier, but he'd made the rules clear and I'd initiated the kiss. If he was going to forget it and I brought it back up, I could get fired. But I wasn't sure that I wanted him to forget it. I didn't like the idea that a kiss that amazing – *two* kisses that amazing – could be so easily forgotten. Unless, of course, they hadn't been good for him. It wasn't like he didn't have a lot to compare them to.

Neither one of us spoke beyond the occasional comment about the food or the weather, and then when our food came, we focused on that. I forced myself to eat even though I didn't really taste anything. I wasn't going to make DeVon mad by ignoring the meal he was paying for. I didn't have a problem getting in his face when he did something wrong, but I wasn't going to be intentionally rude during what could still be considered a business lunch.

Finally, as the waiter brought the check, I couldn't stand the tension anymore. I had to say something. "Shouldn't we talk abo–"

"There's nothing to talk about." He cut me off. "What happened, happened. We can't take it back." He stood up and pulled a hundred dollar bill from his pocket. He tucked it into the slender check holder and gave me a stern look, his eyes cold. "Just don't ever do it again. I never *just* kiss."

I blinked at his final statement and watched as he turned and walked away.

What the hell did that mean?

THIRTY-THREE

DEVON

"So how can I improve my chances of being represented by Mirage Talent?"

The woman asking the question sat across from me, one long leg crossed over the other. She was one of three prospective new clients I was meeting with today, but the only woman.

I raised an eyebrow. "What do you have in mind?"

She smiled at me and I wondered what those ruby-kissed lips would look like stretched around my cock.

"Oh, I think you know, Mr. Ricci. I'd do *anything* to get my career going."

Not exactly a surprising response. I stood up and slowly walked around the desk, letting my gaze run over her. Monique was probably one of the hottest women I'd seen in a long time. Legs that went on for years. Breasts that were a little too perfect to be natural, but had been so well done that only someone like myself would've noticed. She had glossy black hair that framed a model-perfect face and fell just past her shoulders. The perfect length to hold onto while fucking her from behind. Pouting red lips and skin that amazing shade of tan that only Latinas can get without a salon. She had that exotic look that was all the rage now and I could see the heat in her eyes as she enjoyed my perusal. She wanted me to take her and I could already picture all the ways I could. Bent over my desk. Her riding me in my chair. Up against the wall, her hands pinned above her head. The last Latina I'd been with had given me that same look, and I'd needed a three-day hiatus from sex for my dick to recover. Compared to Monique, that last one looked like a five-dollar hooker.

I half-sat, half-leaned on the edge of the desk right in front of her and rested my hands on the expensive wood. "I'm pretty sure we can figure something out. I already have several roles that I can think of off the top of my head that you'll be perfect for."

She leaned forward, giving me an even better view of those magnificent breasts and put her hand on my leg, just above my knee, and gently squeezed. "That's exactly what I need, an agent like you who can give me everything I'm looking for." She ran the tip of her tongue along her bottom lip. "And I do mean *everything*."

Fuck, she was hot.

Her hand slid higher up my leg, and it didn't take a genius to know where she was heading. My cock twitched, and I knew I'd be hard the moment she touched me. Just before she reached her destination, I wrapped my fingers around her wrist.

"As much as I want you to continue – I can't." I didn't recognize the words that were coming out of my mouth.

"Oh." She blinked, confusion clearly showing on her face. "I'm sorry. I didn't know you were involved with someone."

I stood up and lifted my hands, palms out in the universal gesture of surrender. "I'm not." The words came out sharper than I'd intended. What the hell was I doing? "But, if we're going to work together, it would be inappropriate for us to be intimate. That's one of the rules I have in this company." I couldn't believe I'd just said that. I'd never said that to a female client, especially one who looked like Monique.

"Really?" The corners of her mouth curved up into a puzzled smile. "That's *so* not what I heard." She ran her finger across her collarbone to draw attention to her impressive cleavage. "But if you don't think I'm hot enough, you should know that I have a few *very* naughty tricks that might change your mind. But, if you don't want to find out..."

I cleared my throat and made a point of looking at my watch rather than those long legs that I could picture wrapping around my waist. "I have another meeting to attend to, but Bruce will be in touch with you about the paperwork." I gestured towards the door. "I'm looking forward to seeing you again."

"Oh, um, well, thank you," she stammered as I ushered her to the elevator. Her eyes were wide and startled, but I didn't try to offer an explanation. How could I when I didn't understand it myself?

I kept a professional smile on my face until the elevator doors closed, then stalked back to my office and used most of my self-control not to slam the door. I leaned back against it and closed my eyes.

What the fuck was wrong with me?

Monique was exactly my type. Hot, willing and with a self-proclaimed 'naughty' side. She was the kind of woman who, just a few weeks ago, I would already be balls-deep in, making her scream, but as attractive as I thought she was, something inside me had told me to stop. Now that I stopped to analyze it, it felt a lot like guilt, and that made absolutely no sense. Why would I feel guilty about wanting to bang Monique when I'd been through the same scenario dozens of times before?

Krissy's face popped into my head, the look of disgust I'd seen on her face when she'd first seen me in her hotel room. That was followed by the way she'd looked at me yesterday after she'd kissed me. The way she'd tried to use the rules to stop herself. I knew she'd wanted it. I'd felt it when she'd kissed me, when I'd kissed her back, but then she'd pushed me away. She'd tried to hide it, but I'd seen the expression in her eyes, the knowledge of what I was and what I'd do if she let me.

I'd seen the same knowledge in Monique's eyes. In the past, it would've turned me on, knowing I didn't have to worry about complications, but now I couldn't get past it.

I ran a hand through my hair. I hadn't been kidding when I'd told Krissy that this city was made out of tits and ass. Monique had proved that. A lot of the women expected men like me to take advantage of them. Hell, some were even offended if we didn't. My smile was bitter. Monique probably thought I wasn't even hot for her.

I went back to my chair and sat down. I laced my fingertips under my chin. I needed a plan, I decided. I needed to seduce and fuck Krissy before she destroyed me. Fuck her and get her out of my head. Then I could move on and things would get back to normal. Slowly, a plan formed in my head and I chuckled. Perfect.

THIRTY-FOUR

KRISSY

I set the script on my desk as Tracy walked into my office. "I'd like to speak to the assistant casting director for *Blue Monday*." The pilot for Dreamtime TV was easily the best thing I'd read all week. "I want both Cami and Lena to read for the pilot. This would be perfect for either or both of them, and I know it's going to be a hit, so let's make it happen."

Two of the projects I'd gotten them auditions for had ended up going under for lack of financing. Another was stalled, and the rest had gone with other actors. If I could get one or both of them on *Blue Monday*, it would do wonders for their confidence, not to mention mine.

My phone rang a minute later and it was Tracy. "I have Brandy from Dreamtime on the phone for you."

I took a slow breath. I still wasn't quite used to this part of the job. "Put her on the phone please." I used my best 'people person' voice. "Hi, Brandy, this is—"

"I know who you are." The woman's voice was cold as she cut me off. "And you have a lot of balls thinking you can get your clients to read for one of the most anticipated pilots of the season after just two weeks on the job. I realize you're DeVon's new toy, but if you think I'm going to let your little no-talent actresses read for my show, you're sadly mistaken."

I'd always prided myself on having a quick wit and sharp tongue, but I had to admit that the immediate attack had completely caught me off guard. I pulled myself together quickly, ready to tear Brandy to shreds, not only for her referring to me as DeVon's toy but also for calling my clients 'no-talent.' Thinking my boss was a prick was one thing. Hell, I even agreed to that, but basically calling me a whore and then insulting my clients, that was something else. Brandy wasn't waiting for me to respond, however, and the line was dead even as I was opening my mouth.

I slammed the phone down. "What a bitch," I muttered.

"Are you okay?" Tracy's voice came from the doorway. "Can I do anything?"

"I'm fine," I snapped. "Just leave me alone." I immediately felt guilty. "Wait, I'm sorry." She paused in her half-turn towards the door. "I didn't mean to get short with you."

She nodded, and I knew we were okay. I was sure I wasn't the first agent to lose her temper over someone like Brandy. A thought popped into my head.

"Actually, there is one thing you can do."

"Yeah?"

"Get me Brandy's boss on the phone," I said. When in doubt, I thought, go over their head.

"You mean Derrick Johnson?" Tracy looked surprised.

"If he's Brandy's boss, then yes."

"Okay," she said. She started to turn back to her desk.

"What's Derrick's position besides being Brandy's boss?"

"He's the Vice President of Dreamtime."

Well, that explained the surprised look on Tracy's face. That was higher than I'd thought this would go, but I wasn't about to back down now. "That's who I want," I said, as if I'd known all along. "Get him on the phone."

Five minutes later, my phone rang.

"I have Derrick Johnson on the line."

Butterflies suddenly took flight in my stomach, but I kept my voice steady. "Put him through." I heard the familiar click of a call connecting.

"Derrick Johnson."

"Hello, Mr. Johnson." My voice was crisp and professional, betraying none of the nerves I was feeling or my anger at Brady. "This is Krissy Jensen from Mirage Talent. I have two amazing actresses who would be perfect for a role on–"

"Mirage Talent?" he interrupted. "Is that two-time loser DeVon Ricci still running that circus over there?"

Alarm bells went off in my head. "Excuse me?" I managed to stay bright.

"Oh, I guess you don't know the story, do you?" He sounded like he was enjoying himself. "You're new in town, right? That means you never heard what happened to Emma Snow, did you?"

The name wasn't familiar. "Um, no."

"Well, that crazy lunatic boss of yours completely ruined her."

I could hear the anger fueling his enjoyment of sharing the news with someone new.

"She was our prize actress, going to be the next Jennifer Cox, but your perverted boss fucking ruined her with his crazy sex games."

So it wasn't just me he liked to fuck with like that.

Derrick's voice hardened. "It will be a cold day in hell before I let anyone represented by Mirage Talent read for any of my shows. Is that clear, Ms. Jensen?"

The lawyer in me immediately countered, "Well, I'm not DeVon Ricci, and I'm representing two very talented young women who are quality star material. It'd be your loss if you don't at least meet with them." My stomach twisted at what I was going to say next, but it was the only thing I could think of. "And, Mr. Johnson, if you'd do this favor for me, all you'd have to do is let me know what I could do in return."

He was silent for a moment. "What are you implying?"

Bile rose in my throat but I forced it down. "I'd just be very grateful if you overlooked your differences with my boss. I'd owe you."

"Well, now, how can I be sure I can trust you when I call in that favor?" His tone had changed and was now impossible to read.

"We could always discuss it in greater detail once you schedule a reading for my clients. That way, we're each moving towards..." I almost gagged on the words. "Mutual satisfaction."

"Be at my office in twenty minutes. I'll see what I can do for your girls, and we'll further discuss what you can do for me."

As I hung up the phone, the reality of the situation hit me. DeVon had been right when he'd said Hollywood thrived on tits and ass. It wasn't just the actors and actresses who paraded in front of the cameras who were little more than meat. I realized now that DeVon hadn't just been acting like an ass. He'd been preparing me for situations like this. Preparing me for what really went on behind the scenes in the "glamorous" Hollywood film industry.

THIRTY-FIVE

KRISSY

"Mr. Johnson will see you now." The blonde receptionist with the obvious implants, expensive dye job and fake tan waited for me to follow her.

I tried not to show how nervous I was as I stood. I was grateful I'd worn this particular outfit today. It was the right combination of professional and sexy, the kind that got admiring glances from men, but generally not any glares from women. The neckline was low enough that it drew attention to my breasts, but not so low that it was inappropriate. The hemline was fashionable but not flashy, and my four inch heels made my legs look longer than what they were.

I concentrated on the task at hand as I walked after the blonde. I had clients that deserved to be considered for this project, and I was going to do my damnedest to make sure that happened.

The door was open and I walked inside. He was on the phone but motioned for me to take a seat on the couch against the wall. I did and took advantage of the time to observe and try to get a feel for the man I was about to try to charm...and maybe seduce.

The view was gorgeous, at least what I could see of it. We were at the top of one of the few skyscrapers on the west side and I wondered how far I could see. The windows were floor to ceiling and there was nothing blocking out the bright California sun. Everything in the office spoke of power and money. Typical of a man in Derrick Johnson's position.

As for the man himself, he was pretty close to what I'd imagined. Mid-forties, slender without a hint of a gut. He was handsome, but in the kind of way that made me think he'd had a bit of work done. Not enough to be too obvious, but enough that he probably looked like a cousin to his younger self. His hair was cut short, but still couldn't disguise the fact that it was thinning. It was black, without a trace of gray, though I suspected that was thanks to his stylist. After all, appearances were everything in Hollywood and only certain kinds of men could pull off the salt-and-pepper look.

He hung up the phone and came over to sit in the armchair next to the couch. I gave him my full attention, knowing that men like him enjoyed nothing more than thinking that a woman was completely entranced by them.

"Krissy Jensen," he said. "I've heard a thing or two about you."

With George Hamilton out there running his mouth, I didn't doubt it.

"In fact," Derrick continued. "Rumor has it that you're the next golden girl of Hollywood agents."

I raised an eyebrow. I didn't believe for a moment that's what he'd heard. For one, it sounded too much like a come-on. Second, I already knew how people in the industry were looking at me. I decided honesty was the right way to go in this particular situation.

"Really? That's not what I heard." I crossed my ankles and shifted so that I was angled towards Derrick. "In fact, one of your casting directors, Brandy, called me 'DeVon's new toy.'"

Derrick gave one of those laughs that was too charming to be real. "I do apologize for Brandy's comment." He shook his head slightly, as if he'd had to scold a child who'd been impolite in public. "You do have to realize, though, that DeVon isn't exactly the most admired person around here." He quickly clarified. "Not that he isn't a great agent. He is, but his personal sexual preferences and behavior are notorious." Derrick's expression was shrewd, like he was gauging my reaction. "He ruins the women that he takes to bed."

I gave him a tight smile, and let it express my doubts.

"Believe what you want," Derrick said, reading me correctly. "But sooner or later, you'll find out just how much of a bastard DeVon really is." He gave himself a little shake, as if getting rid of all the negative things we were discussing. "Enough about that. Let's talk about what you came here for. You wanted me to look at someone."

I handed him Cami's and Lena's files. "There are a couple different parts I was thinking they might be good for. Jennifer, Cassidy, Beverly, and maybe Dawn if you wanted to go a different direction."

He studied each of the files without saying anything and that made me feel good. That meant he was taking my request seriously. "We've already cast Beverly and have a pretty good idea of who we want for Cassidy. We are going a different direction with Dawn, but your ladies won't work since we're changing her to a him."

I tried not to let the disappointment show.

"But, I do like this Cami. There's something about her."

I smiled despite wanting to look cool and aloof.

"I agree that she has the potential to be Jennifer." He closed the files and handed them back to me. "I'll let her read for it."

"Thank you," I said sincerely. "You won't regret it."

"Now," he said. "You'd mentioned that if I gave one of your clients a shot, you'd be willing to return the favor. What, exactly, are you willing to do now that I've kept my side of things?"

I shifted in my seat. Here was the part I hadn't wanted to think about. I glanced down at Derrick's hand and saw a band on his left hand. That could be my out if I played it right. I gave him a half-smile. "Like I said, you can just let me know what you'd like me to do, but we definitely don't want to upset a certain someone." I gestured towards his hand.

"Oh, this?" He held up his hand. "I'm a widower. Just never got used to going without the ring so I haven't taken it off."

I swallowed hard. Shit. There went my easy out.

"You can relax."

He smiled at me but it didn't put me at ease. His next words, however, did make me warier.

"I'm not trying to get you to fuck me or anything like that." He leaned back in the chair. "I'm not like your boss."

I ignored the insult towards DeVon, and waited for the other shoe to drop.

"There is, however, something you can do for me."

Here it came. "What's that?" I asked.

"Get me information," Derrick said. "Tell me what DeVon is up to. Which screenplays have his interest. Any new clients. Like I said, I can't talk to the bastard, but I would sure like to know his comings and goings."

I kind of wished he'd just asked for a blowjob. I wanted to get Cami a chance to read for this part, especially since I was sure that they'd all love her as soon as they heard her, but I couldn't double-cross my boss, no matter what I thought of him. I didn't do that. I'd been stabbed in the back before, and I wasn't about to do that, not unless DeVon did it first. Besides, I wanted to make it in this town, not completely burn the bridges I'd made. Derrick must've sensed some of that about me since he'd been trying to run DeVon down with all of the comments about how he treated women, but I could tell that he wasn't entirely sure what I'd say.

The thing was, I wasn't going to refuse. In fact, I had a plan. I nodded. "Agreed. I'll see what I can do."

The surprised look on his face said that Derrick hadn't expected me to go through with it. "Excellent," he said. "I'll have

Brandy contact you to set up the read for Cami." He held out his hand, gripping mine for a few seconds longer than necessary. "I look forward to seeing you again...very soon."

I resisted the urge to wipe my hand on my dress as I stood, and I was glad I did because Derrick leaned in close, putting his mouth next to my ear.

"It's not that I don't want to fuck your brains out, but I don't like sloppy seconds."

My chest tightened and I took a step back. I spoke in the most sugary-sweet voice I could muster. "Not that it's any of your business, but I've never fucked DeVon." The smile I was wearing was forced, as was the expression on my face as I gave Derrick a look over. "Such a shame you had to jump to conclusions. I would've loved playing around with you."

Before he could respond, I spun on my heel and walked away as fast as I could without looking like I was running. My temper was boiling and hot tears pricked at my eyelids. I wasn't sure if they were because I was hurt or because I was furious. Either one was a viable option.

I'd actually thought Derrick was going to be a good guy. That he was going to prove that DeVon was the exception and not the rule. I'd actually been foolish enough to believe that he was all about business, even if he had been asking me to spy on DeVon. Then he threw all of that away and showed his true colors. At least DeVon didn't hide his intentions or couch propositions in lewd insults.

I shook my head as I slid into the driver's seat of my car. DeVon was better looking that Derrick and could have any woman he wanted, but did that really make him any better than Derrick, simply because he was hotter? Wasn't he just using women for sex, too? Who was I kidding, entertaining the idea that DeVon could actually have feelings for me?

At least I didn't actually like him, I told myself. I was just attracted to him physically, and who could blame me? The man

196 M. S. PARKER

was walking, talking, breathing sex. An asshole, yes, but hot as hell. I didn't want anything but a good lay. That's what I needed, I decided, to set things straight. I needed to get him out of my system.

I needed to fuck him.

The memory of his lips on mine hit me and my hands clenched the steering wheel.

The sooner, the better.

THIRTY-SIX

DEVON

My focus was totally shot.

Ever since Krissy had kissed me, I couldn't look at a nice ass or tits without thinking about her, and in my business, that meant I spent way too much time thinking about her.

It would be over soon, I reassured myself. It had to be. I had to stop thinking about that kiss.

As much as I hated how it was constantly on my mind, the kiss had been amazing. I could always tell from just one kiss what the sex would be like with someone. I'd had my predictions proven right time and again, and this time I knew that when it happened between me and her, it would be amazing. And then it'd be over. I'd fuck her hard, use her, and then reassign her to work under Bruce or Clark. She'd be their problem then, and if they made a move, so much the better.

I just needed to get back to my usual groove, and fast. I didn't think it'd take much to get her into bed. We only needed the right situation, and as I looked down at the pair of tickets on my desk, I knew exactly what that situation would be.

"Melissa," I hit the intercom.

"Yes, Mr. Ricci?"

"Contact Ms. Jensen and let her know not to make any plans for Friday evening. She'll be coming with me to the *Underside* premiere."

"Yes, Sir."

That should do the trick, I thought as I ran my fingers over the tickets. This would be Krissy's first genuine movie premiere and she'd be thrilled with me for taking her to such an exclusive event. I doubted she wanted to see the new Sledgehammer action movie, but all the stars would be there and I'd make sure she met them all. Later, at the after party, after she'd spent the night rubbing elbows with the epitome of who's who in Hollywood, I'd make my move.

It was a perfect plan.

THIRTY-SEVEN

KRISSY

When Melissa had called and told me not to make plans for Friday evening, I'd had a moment of wild hope that DeVon was taking me out. Then she'd told me that it was a movie premiere which meant all business, and I hadn't been sure whether I was disappointed or relieved. I'd thanked her and let myself focus on the excitement of getting to attend something so big.

It had been hard to concentrate the rest of the day, and my nerves had been on edge when I'd seen DeVon out of the corner of my eye as we were both walking towards the front doors. I'd slowed instinctively, and he'd fallen in step beside me.

"So, about Friday," I'd begun.

"Movie premieres are a great place to mingle and network," he'd said with barely a glance towards me. "Make sure you look your best."

I resisted the urge to tell him that I wasn't stupid. I'd seen enough coverage to know that movie premieres were a big deal. People dressed up as if it were the Oscars or something. That, plus the fact that DeVon had felt the need to reiterate that I needed to look my best had meant that just any old dress wouldn't do. I'd started to suspect that the reason Mirage paid so well was because of how much we had to spend on clothes. I'd taken out my credit card, one that was now dangerously close to being maxed out, and bought a sexy evening gown.

Now, as I stood in front of my building, watching a limo pull up to the curb, I was starting to wonder if I'd made a mistake. The dress was by some designer I'd never heard of, but I loved it anyway. The hem brushed against my toes, but the slit in the side went to well above the middle of my thigh. The neckline plunged so much that I'd actually thought I'd need to tape the material to my boobs so that things stayed where they were supposed to. The last thing I needed was a wardrobe malfunction, but, in the end, I hadn't needed anything extra. The material was rich but the design was simple and it clung to me like a second skin. Still, I felt vastly overdressed as I slid into the backseat.

DeVon glanced at me and gave me a look that said he approved, but nothing more. We rode in silence and when we got in line to be dropped off, I started to watch the other women who were heading down the carpet. My previous thoughts of being overdressed now felt stupid. I didn't see a single dress that wasn't at least a several thousand dollar designer gown.

DeVon leaned over until his arm brushed against mine, sending tingles of electricity through me. "Your choice for tonight is impeccable. Much better than those over-inflated haute couture dresses that do absolutely nothing but say that money has been spent." He gestured towards a woman who was wearing what looked like a triangular piece of aluminum foil.

It didn't take a genius to know that it was a typical 'sensational' piece, created to attract attention to the dress and the designer rather than to flatter the woman wearing it.

I smiled at him, but didn't say anything because the limo was at the front of the line now and the door was opening. DeVon got out first, and then offered me his hand. I took it and tried not to think about the strength in those fingers as he helped me from the vehicle...or the disappointment when he let me go.

I didn't have much time to dwell on it as cameras started flashing, blinding me. DeVon put his hand on the small of my back as he steered me through the throng on the red carpet. Journalists and fans yelled from the sidelines and someone asked if I was DeVon's girlfriend. I didn't hear him respond, but that could've just been because I was trying not to think about how good it felt to have his hand on me and how glad I was that I'd gone with a dress with such a low cut back that half of his hand was on bare skin. A shiver went through me as he led me into the theater, with him smiling and greeting people the entire way.

"Charlie!" He clapped his free hand on the shoulder of a handsome, middle-aged man that I recognized as being last year's Oscar nominee for Best Director. I thought he should've won, but then again, I usually disagreed with most of the Emmy and Oscar wins.

"DeVon, how've you been?" The man beamed.

"Not as good as you, I hear," DeVon gestured to a slender, much younger man who was standing next to Charlie.

"I don't know, DeVon, you've got quite the looker there, too," Charlie said as he reached for the hand of the young man.

"Krissy Jensen, meet Charlie Irons and his husband, Nathan."

I put out a hand and shook with both Charlie and Nathan.

"Krissy here is my new hot-shot assistant. She's got the goods, gentleman," DeVon said without a trace of sarcasm.

Charlie raised an eyebrow. "That's quite a compliment coming from you." He looked at me. "DeVon here helped me cast Gracie Bevins as Zara in *The King's Fool*."

"Really?" I looked at DeVon, impressed. "She was amazing. I couldn't imagine anyone else playing Zara."

"Krissy's eye is just as good," DeVon said. "She's an up and comer."

His praise was easing the knot in my stomach, and as it continued each time he introduced me to someone new, I found myself beginning to relax and even join in the conversation. I kept waiting for him to add in something about me having a bad attitude or anything that could make something negative out of all of the nice things he was saying, but it never happened. This was a side of DeVon I'd never seen before.

He was charming, and not in a "trying to get laid" kind of way. He joked and flirted, but was never too much. And he was actually very attentive to me, making sure I was never left out of the conversation or left behind. Each time we moved on, he'd put his hand back where it had been, and gently steer me to whoever was the next person on his list. When I shivered again, he asked if I was cold and offered his jacket. I politely declined, and hoped he thought the flush in my cheeks was from nerves rather from the fact that I couldn't tell him that the shiver was from his touch and not the weather. The next time a waitress went by with glasses of champagne, he grabbed one for me and that helped take the last of the edge off.

As we headed for our seats, we chatted about mundane things that seemed relevant to the situation. Favorite movies and directors. Which casting choices had been brilliant and which ones we wished we'd had a shot to try. Surprisingly, we agreed on almost all of them. Almost. I was still trying to convince him that Lucas Freeman would've been better as the lead in *Write Home Sometime* when the lights dimmed.

It had been a while since I'd been to the theater, and even longer still since I'd been there with a man. I'd forgotten how, when the darkness settled and the movie began, it was easy to forget the people nearby. I'd also forgotten that, no matter how posh the theater, the seats were still close together and, as I leaned away from the man on my right who kept trying to look down the front of my dress, my arm pressed against DeVon's. I felt him stiffen, and the tension between us suddenly ratcheted up several notches. I moved back so that I wasn't touching either of the men sitting next to me, but it didn't stop whatever it was that was growing between DeVon and I. I didn't know if he felt it, too, but I hardly paid any attention to the movie because I was trying very hard not to touch him.

Then, the movie was ending and the lights were coming back on. People were clapping so I joined in, even though I didn't remember a single thing from the film. Not that it was my kind of movie anyway, but others seemed to have liked it.

"I need a drink," DeVon said. For a moment, I thought he was angry, but when I looked, he was smiling at me. "Something stronger than champagne."

"Okay," I said slowly.

"There's a fridge in the limo," he said. "Why don't we head that way, and we can get something on our way to the after party."

"The what?"

DeVon grinned. "Did I forget to mention that? Oops."

I laughed. I couldn't help it. The smile wasn't lecherous or smug or any of the other things I'd come to associate with DeVon's smiles. Instead, it was the kind of grin that showed me what he must've looked like when he'd been little. I liked this side of DeVon, more than I cared to admit.

"How about I make us both a vodka martini?" DeVon suggested as we got back into the limo.

I agreed and watched him mix the drink with an ease that made me wonder if he'd been a bartender at some point. I'd seen enough bartenders to know how they worked. And by 'seen,' I meant slept with.

It was strong, and exactly what I needed. I was actually having fun and I didn't want anything ruining tonight.

"So, where's this after party?" I asked after I'd finished half of my drink.

"Brentwood," DeVon answered. "Steven Morrison's mansion."

I knew the name. He'd directed the movie we'd seen tonight. I just hoped he didn't ask me what I'd thought of it. Then I realized that I didn't just know the name because of tonight's movies. Even back in New York, I'd known the name. Morrison was notorious for his parties. There was always great food, plenty of alcohol and dozens of drop-dead gorgeous models who mingled with the guests.

I gulped down the rest of my drink. I had a feeling I was going to need even more before the night was over. This party would be the perfect opportunity for me to move on with my plan of having sex with DeVon to get him out of my system. Why put off until tomorrow what I could do tonight? Or, more accurately, *who* I wanted to do tonight.

THIRTY-EIGHT

DEVON

The drive from Hollywood took forever. I'd always loved the view, but tonight, I just wanted to get to the house. Some things were more beautiful than the scenery. As we finally topped the last summit point, we were at Mandeville Canyon. I looked over at Krissy who was staring at the view.

"I love these houses," I said. "But the drive is ridiculous."

As we got out of the limo and the music from the party reached us, I forgot all about the drive. It was time to show Krissy what it was really all about. What *I* was really all about. She'd seen me at work, and I knew the kind of vibe I gave there. Now she needed to see how I could schmooze all these people, how I could charm any of them into pretty much anything. She needed to know that I didn't just flirt with women to get laid. I wined and dined everyone in the industry to get what I wanted. Male, female. Directors, producers, actors, casting directors, all of them.

A few of the junior executives from various production companies were standing outside the house and I greeted them by name. Out of the corner of my eye, I caught Krissy looking surprised, then impressed. I didn't blame her. Not many people in my position would bother to learn the names of anyone but those at the top. I'd built my company with hard work and charm, and the latter worked even better when it started at the bottom. This mentality had helped me build Mirage into what it was today. A surge of pride went through me.

"Wow," Krissy breathed as she took in the entire picture.

I knew she came from money – I'd done my research, after all – but I also knew that this kind of party wasn't like anything she'd seen back home. The house reminded me of Howard Leffner's place. I'd only been there once. I'd gotten the impression he hadn't taken too kindly to me fucking a couple of his girls since he'd never asked me back. All right, technically, there had been four of them, but in my defense, they'd started it.

Half of the guests were inside dancing and drinking, the other half outside by the pool where dozens of bikini-clad models were hanging out. Some were in the water, others on rafts. All around were middle-aged men practically coming in their pants watching the girls bounce around. A few of those I recognized as VIPs already had a couple girls hanging on their arms. There were even a handful of young men in skimpy shorts for the straight women and gay men. Morrison didn't discriminate.

The two of us walked into the house and I kept the same strategy as I'd had at the premiere. Greet people, charm them, and use every opportunity I had to touch Krissy. Back at the theater, when we'd gotten out of the limo, I'd automatically put my hand on her back to move her through the crowd. I hadn't realized that the cut of her dress would put her bare skin under my fingers, and I'd actually had to take a few seconds to will away my body's natural response. Once I'd gotten over the surprise, I'd found myself touching her again and again, even when it had become obvious that she was more comfortable. Now, I put my hand on her back, but this time, I let the tips of my fingers slide under the side material. I heard her catch her breath and the fire that had been smoldering inside me ignited. It was time to move in for the kill.

I leaned down as if the music was too loud for her to hear me over it and spoke in her ear. "Did you know that from outside, you can see the whole west side of LA?"

She turned her head just enough so that our faces were even closer together, but not so much that we were touching. "Show me everything."

I really hoped I wasn't imaging the double meaning in those words. I'd spent almost the entire movie thinking about all of the things I wanted to do to her. By the time the credits had started to roll, I'd been certain I'd need to excuse myself to the restroom just to alleviate some of the tension.

The two of us walked towards the set of French doors that led out back, but before we could get to them, someone stepped in front of us. I nearly cursed, but forced myself to bite the words back. Harlan Rickard was a director whose only claim to fame was *Into the Darkness*, a film that had actually managed to make money and get awards – fifteen years ago. He'd delivered flop after flop ever since, pieces of shit that were neither entertaining nor insightful. Still, he managed to get invited to parties, and he generally spent his time telling anyone who'd listen about his 'next big thing,' and trying to get naïve actresses into bed.

"DeVon," he slurred. The glass in his hand was obviously not his first of the night. "Just the man I was looking for."

I suddenly had a very bad idea where this was going to go. Harlan took a step towards me and when he spoke again, it was all I could do to keep from gagging. His breath reeked of liquor, tobacco and something so foul that I almost felt bad for the guy. Almost.

"I've decided that I'm going to let you represent me."

The hand not on Krissy's back curled into a fist. I wasn't fond of people I liked telling me what I was going to do, much less people I couldn't stand. "Is that so?" I kept my tone mild.

"I've been thinking about changing agencies for a while," he said. "Margo used to be the hottest thing in town, but she's getting old and I need someone new. Someone like you. Someone who can convince these studios of what they're missing by not hiring me."

If Krissy hadn't been standing next to me, I would've had a couple things to say to Harlan about why he hadn't done any decent work in fifteen years, but I was trying very hard to get Krissy to see me in a different light. If I could respond politely to this asshole, it might go a long way to making this work tonight.

"I'm sure Margo can make a chance to retain her number one client." I gave myself a pat on the back for not smirking when I said it. Everyone knew Margo wanted to dump him.

He shook his head. "Bitch keeps trying to pawn me off on some underlings, and half the time she won't take my calls. No, I need someone who understands that I require special attention. A guy like me needs the top dog available twenty-four seven, all resources focused on me. If she'd been doing her job half that good, I'd be directing the new Dramer film instead of that asshole, Merlyn."

I turned my laugh into a cough. I needed to get out of here before the heat that had been generating with Krissy burned out. "Tell you what, Harlan. Why don't you let me talk to a few people, and then we can sit down as see what Mirage can do for you."

"Excellent." Harlan clapped me on the arm, then looked over at Krissy. "I'll be expecting for her to be one of the perks."

Before I could lose my temper and knock his teeth down his fucking throat, Harlan staggered away. I took a slow, deep breath, then looked down at Krissy. "Sorry about that. Some people are just..."

"Dicks?" She supplied.

I laughed, a genuine laugh to my surprise. "I was going to say desperate, but that works, too."

"Yeah, desperate is also accurate." She paused, then asked, "Are you really going to have a meeting with him?"

I rolled my eyes. "Are you high? Of course not. I wouldn't even be able to get that guy a job cleaning the set of a porn film."

She laughed, and the sound sparked that fire in me again. I wondered what other sounds she was going to make tonight.

"So, about that view?"

I offered her my arm. I would've preferred to keep my hand on her back, but I was trying to repair the damage Harlan had done and a bit of sweet humor was better for that. "If you'll come with me, my lady."

This time, she rolled her eyes, but she took my arm and the two of us went through the doorway and out onto the patio and pool area. The pool itself was impressive, with a waterfall coming down from a rock structure at the back. It flowed into a river that then carried the water into what had been designed to look like a jungle lagoon. Not my taste, but excellent architecture, I had to admit.

Not surprisingly, several of the women in the pool had already mysteriously lost their tops. I could feel Krissy watching me as my eyes skimmed over the women and moved on without lingering on any of them. I probably would've ignored them even if I hadn't been trying to seduce Krissy. Fake tits didn't generally do it for me, especially the ones currently on display. If you're going to get them, at least make sure they're proportional to the rest of your body.

No, I thought, there was only one pair of breasts I wanted to see tonight.

I led Krissy away from the activity and noise and over to a little, secluded alcove overlooking Mandeville Canyon. The view was spectacular and the location private enough that I knew we wouldn't be interrupted. Krissy wasn't the first woman I'd brought here. I'd even fucked a couple while admiring the view. I didn't plan on that for Krissy, though. As much as I knew I had to fuck her so I could get my head on straight, I liked her enough that I wasn't going to just have a quickie right here. Since we were only getting one night, I wanted to be able to take my time. I wanted to make her scream my name.

Now that we were here, though, I was suddenly unsure of what to do next. If she'd been one of my usual women, I'd just get her on her knees and have her blow me to get things started. If she'd been some empty-headed bimbo, I'd just grab her and kiss her. A little bit of groping and we'd be ready to go. But she wasn't either of those things. Krissy was intelligent and strong. If I pushed too hard, I could ruin everything.

Well, there was one thing I knew she hadn't objected to. I unwound my arm from hers and put my hand on her back again. This time, however, instead of just keeping it there, I let my fingers start to move over her skin. Lightly, nothing too suggestive. Little tingles of electricity moved up my fingers and arm, and I swallowed hard. What was that all about?

I didn't have time to think about it because Krissy was moving. For a second, I thought she was pulling away from me, but that wasn't it. She was actually turning towards me, closing the gap until we were only inches apart. Her heels made her tall enough that, while she still had to tilt her head to look at me, it wasn't an awkward angle.

"Are you going to kiss me soon? Otherwise, I'm going to go fucking nuts."

My eyebrows went up. I hadn't been expecting that response. I wasn't about to overthink it, though.

Our mouths crashed together, and my hand flexed on her back as I pulled her tight against me. Her hands slid across my chest, and I buried my free hand in her hair. My teeth scraped her bottom lip, and she moaned, her hands sliding around my back and then down to my hips. I slid my tongue into her mouth, and she did the same. Then, she lightly bit my lip, and a bolt of pleasure went straight through me. I pulled back, suddenly hard as a rock. What the hell? Kissing was nice and all, but we hadn't gotten done anything that should've made me feel like I was about to come in my pants. I'd never had that happen from a fully-clothed, no groping kiss.

I looked down at her. Her lips were still slightly parted and her eyes closed, as if she was savoring the kiss. My stomach twisted as I read the desire and passion on her face. My breath was coming faster and my heart was pounding, but it wasn't from the kiss. Feelings were welling up inside of me, ones that I'd thought I'd gotten rid of for good. I liked that I'd made her moan. I liked the way she felt in my arms and that she wanted me, but it wasn't the way I liked it with other women. It wasn't about the power I had over them. She made me feel like I was something special, and it had been a very long time since a woman had made me feel that way.

I couldn't do it. As much as I wanted her, I couldn't go through with my original plan to fuck her, then pawn her off on one of my associates. She reminded me too much of...*her*. The woman I'd loved and lost. A surge of protectiveness washed over me, strong enough to make me step back. I didn't want to do anything that would hurt her, and if we fucked tonight, no matter how discreet we'd try to be, it'd get out and everyone would say that the rumors of her sleeping her way into the job were true. I couldn't do that to her.

Fuck it all. I actually cared.

THIRTY-NINE

KRISSY

What the hell had just happened? That kiss had been amazing. All a girl could ask for, and the promise of everything I wanted before the night was over. I'd felt him hard against my hip, so I knew he'd been enjoying it, too. Why, then, had he stopped? I was ready and willing. What was he waiting for? I was sure he'd wanted this, too, and I knew I had to fuck him to get him out of my system or I was going to go crazy.

I was trying very hard not to make too much of that and him putting on the brakes wasn't helping things. He was smoking hot, so I knew there was the whole physical factor, but my entire MO was to fuck good-looking guys, then split once my itch got scratched. The only ones I ever stayed with beyond the first fuck or two had money, but none of those were as hot as DeVon. Granted, he had the body and the money, but there was no way in hell I wanted a relationship with him.

And I knew he was the same way as me. He fucked and dashed. He wasn't the relationship type. The man had invited me to have a foursome with him the first time we'd met, for fuck's sake!

So why the hell was he acting like some prude all of a sudden. I looked down at myself. He hadn't even tried to touch my boobs or my ass at all tonight. Was there something wrong with the way I looked? I'd seen the topless women with the huge fake tits. I didn't compare to them. Was that what he liked? I'd thought he'd pretty much ignored them, but maybe I'd been wrong.

I thought about going in for another kiss, but instead just sighed. I wasn't going to let him off easy by throwing myself at him. Sure, I wanted to fuck, but I wasn't about to waste my time if he wasn't interested.

"What's wrong?" I asked bluntly.

His eyes met mine, and he said the last thing I ever would've expected. "Be patient. This is new territory with me. I need more time."

What the hell was he talking about? New territory? We were going to fuck. Meaningless, hot sex. Nothing he hadn't done hundreds of times before. And now he wanted to take it slow? I seriously hoped he meant that he wanted to draw it out, like some exquisite torture, because that was the only possibility I was willing to entertain. Thinking that he might want something more wasn't something I wanted to even consider.

I gave him my best sultry smile. The music from the house changed and I got an idea. "Maybe this will help you decide."

I took his right hand and put it on my lower back, resisting the urge to move it lower onto my ass. I wasn't going to be quite that brazen. I'd rather do seductive than slutty. I took his other hand and began to move to the slow, sensual music. I kept distance between our bodies at first, letting the heat build as one song bled into another. Only then did I slide my hand from his, forcing him to put his hand on my waist. I moved my hand up his arm until both of my hands met behind his neck. I closed the space between us and leaned in, kissing him gently. It was just a brush of my lips against his so I could gauge his reaction.

Nothing.

I struggled not to scowl. If I'd done that to any other guy, he'd be grabbing me and trying for something more.

I tried again, pressing my mouth harder against his and parting my lips in a blatant invitation.

Still nothing.

I was starting to go from horny to pissed.

I decided to try something a little less subtle and let my body move to the music, rubbing against him as I took his mouth again. This time, I pushed my tongue between his lips.

His hands tightened around my waist.

Finally, a reaction!

Then he was pulling me against him, his lips forcing mine wider, and I gave myself over to the kiss. Whatever hesitation he'd been trying for was lost as he devoured my mouth, possessing it completely. My fingers curled in the hair at the nape of his neck and I moaned as I imagined what it would feel like against my thighs. He finally broke the kiss, but kept our bodies molded together and rested his forehead against mine.

"Fuck time." His voice was rough. "I don't need time. Let's get out of here."

"I don't think I can wait that long." The ache between my legs throbbed in agreement. It had been a long time since I'd met a man who held the kind of potential DeVon did. I took a step back and crooked my finger at him. "Come on, let's explore upstairs." I grinned at him. "It could be a little dangerous, and I like danger." I turned and started walking towards the house. After just a couple steps, I looked over my shoulder and raised an eyebrow. I didn't even bother to try to hide my double-entendre. "Are you coming?"

FORTY

DEVON

Was she fucking kidding? Of course I was coming. And I fully intended that to be true in both definitions of the word by the end of the night. There was a part of me that wanted to take it slow, make it something that I was terrified it could be, but I wasn't an idiot. No man could say no to an offer like that.

We walked quickly back to the main room, not touching, but so aware of each other's presence that it was like a nearly painful buzz of electricity across my skin. As soon as we reached the door, I saw a problem. The room was packed and every person we passed would expect us to stop and greet them. That's what we were there for, after all. If we blew anyone off, it'd be weeks of damage control and more fuel for the fire. The last thing I wanted to do was draw attention to what Krissy and I were about to do, and the second worst thing would be for us to have to wait. My body was already responding to the thought of what was to come and if I went inside, things had the potential to be very awkward and embarrassing, even for me.

Fortunately, I knew there was another way. I took her arm and tried not to think about the way her skin hummed against mine. "Let's go in here." I led her through a nearly invisible door to the right.

The door took us into the kitchen. While we received several startled looks from personnel preparing various finger foods, none of them told us to leave. I ignored them and snatched a small tray of finger rolls, then, with a wink at Krissy, grabbed a bottle of champagne from the fridge. She laughed, the sound going straight to my cock. As we passed by a waiter filling glasses with sparkling liquid, I snagged two glasses and hurried away before anyone could complain about my theft.

The next door took us to a large dining room. It was empty and the thought of grabbing her, throwing her onto the table and having my way with her right then was almost too tempting. Only the knowledge that we'd never be alone long enough to do half of what I had planned kept me moving.

"That way." Krissy pointed towards one of the doors at the other end of the room.

She was a step ahead of me, but only because I wanted to watch her ass as she walked in those amazing heels. The door opened to a long hallway and we went down it. I was starting to think that fucking her on the massive dining room table was a good idea after all when we finally reached a staircase.

She put her foot on the step, but stopped when I reached out with my free hand and grabbed her wrist. I pulled her close to me, balancing my full hand to the side so I could bend my head close enough to inhale the intoxicating scent that was her. "Are you sure you want to do this?" I asked. "There's no going back after this." I had to know, because there was no way I'd want to stop if we went any further.

She looked up at me, her eyes dark pools of lust. A knot in my stomach tightened. Those fucking beautiful eyes.

"I'm sure," she said. She pushed herself up until I thought she was going to kiss me, but instead, she sucked my bottom lip into her mouth. She held it there for just a moment before biting down hard enough to send a jolt straight through me, then released it. She took off up the stairs, laughing while I stared for a moment before practically running after her.

She was going to be the death of me.

When we reached the top of the stairs, I yanked open the first door I saw, fully intending to throw her through it and have my way with her.

It was a closet.

"That might be a tight fit," Krissy said with a laugh.

I growled at her and that just made her laugh even more. She didn't even bother with the next door, but instead headed for the double doors at the end of the hallway like she owned the place. Damn, that confidence was sexy!

She pushed open the doors and I peered over her head. It was a massive bedroom and, right in the very center was the biggest bed I'd ever seen. It was red, round, and obviously meant to hold more than two people. I knew where we were, but I wasn't about to let that stop me. I set what I was carrying down on an expensive-looking table that sat next to the door and then turned to close it. When I did, I noticed something that didn't really surprise me, considering what I knew about the exhibitionist owner of this bedroom.

"There's no lock."

"Good."

I wasn't able to hide my startled expression at Krissy's reply and she smiled at me.

"The possibility of getting caught just makes it more fun."

The more time I spent with her, the more I liked her.

She slowly walked towards me, the sway of her hips fighting with her breasts and eyes for my attention. My entire body tensed in anticipation of her touching me, but she didn't. Instead, she reached past me and picked up the food I'd brought up. I hadn't really paid attention to what was on the tray, but apparently, they were a dessert and not a sandwich. A cookie of some kind wrapped around cream frosting. I didn't know what it was called, but I didn't think it was supposed to turn me on.

Krissy, however, managed to make it do just that. She ran the tip of her tongue along her bottom lip, wetting it, and then flicked it out to catch just a dab of the frosting.

"Yum." She licked another bit of frosting from the cookie and I had to bite back a moan. She used her finger to scoop out some and held it out to me. I opened my mouth and let her slip the digit inside.

The sweet burst across my tastebuds, mingled with something that was uniquely her. I swirled my tongue around her finger, thoroughly cleaning it, my eyes locked with hers the entire time. When she withdrew her finger from my mouth, she ran it down my chest, following the line of my tie.

"Delicious." I was surprised at how hoarse my voice was.

"Want to know a secret?" she asked as she loosened my tie. She leaned closer when I nodded and lowered her voice even though we were the only two in the room. "I taste better."

Fuck.

My tie landed on the floor before I realized she'd undone it, and her fingers were already working their way through my buttons. I had to slow things down or I wasn't going to be able to enjoy this as much as I wanted to. I turned away from her and poured us each a glass of champagne. The few minutes it took were enough for me to regain my composure. I handed her a glass.

"To new beginnings." The words were out of my mouth before I'd had a chance to think them through. What the hell? I took a larger gulp of my drink than I'd intended.

Fortunately, Krissy didn't seem fazed by what I'd said, but instead added her own part to the toast. "And to sexual pleasures."

I drank again to that.

I had just set my glass down when Krissy's hands were on my shirt again. This time, she didn't bother with the buttons and just pulled. Some came free while others popped off. I didn't care because then she was pushing the shirt from my shoulders and her hands were running over my chest and abs, her eyes almost black with the intensity of her desire. My skin felt like it was on fire as she explored every inch of my toned body. When she pressed her mouth against the space just above my bellybutton, I had to close my eyes as a surge of heat when straight to my cock. I'd never gotten so hard, so fast as I did when I was with her.

When her hands went to my belt, I opened my eyes. I wanted to see her reaction. I'd always heard how I measured up to other men, but I also knew that Krissy wasn't like other women. She wouldn't lie to me just because she thought it was what I wanted to hear.

She grinned up at me as her hands did their thing. She tucked her fingers under the waistband at my hips, sliding under the elastic of my underwear as well, and, in one smooth motion, pulled everything down to mid-thigh.

Her eyes widened. "Holy fuck!"

FORTY-ONE

KRISSY

I've seen a lot of cocks. I mean, I'm not a slut, but still, I've seen a lot since my first. I've seen ones I didn't even want to touch, and others that I couldn't wait to get inside me. Thin, thick, long, short, curved, straight. And, with total honesty, I could say that I'd never seen one that made me instantly and completely wet like DeVon's did. He was about an inch longer than average, so I'd fucked a couple that were longer, but none of them had been that thick. Some girls may like the guys who're so big it feels like they're gonna come out of their mouth. I didn't. I liked the ones who could rub every single inch of me, and DeVon looked like he could deliver that in spades. I'd felt him hard when we'd kissed, but that hadn't even come close to doing him justice. My mouth watered at the thought of him pushing past my lips...

"Krissy."

The amusement in his voice told me that he'd said my name more than once.

I tore my gaze away and looked up. His eyes were sparkling,

but the moment I wrapped my hand as far as it would go around him, they closed and his head fell back.

"Fuck," he groaned.

I grinned. I loved it when men made that sound, and I loved knowing that I caused it. I released him and took a step back. He started to protest, but the words died in his throat when he saw me unzipping my dress. I was suddenly very glad that I hadn't needed to tape the dress to my breasts. That would've made my sexy little striptease a bit awkward.

The heat in his eyes went through me as he ran his gaze down my body. Because of the kind of dress it was, I hadn't worn a bra, and the way it had hugged my body meant a thong if I wanted to avoid a pantyline, so as the material pooled around my feet, all I was left wearing were my thigh-highs and a tiny piece of black silk that was rapidly getting soaked.

He let out a string of what I could only assume were curse words in Italian. Then again, it could've been a shopping list, for all I knew, and it still would've made me want to go to my knees.

And while I fully intended to have that magnificent piece of flesh in my mouth at some point, I had other things in mind to get started. Besides, he needed to cool off a bit if this was going to last as long as I hoped we both wanted it to. I backed towards the bed and climbed onto it without taking my eyes off of him. It had taken me a while to get that ability down pat. I'd fallen off of more beds than I cared to admit.

When I was comfortably propped up in the center on a pillow that the owner of this fabulous room had so kindly left in the middle of the bed for me, I crooked my finger at DeVon and beckoned him. He started to take a step, then realized that his pants were around his thighs. While he was getting out of them and his shoes, I toed my shoes off. I didn't know if he preferred women to keep heels on during sex, but I didn't care. I'd keep on my thigh-highs if he wanted me to, but the shoes were going. Toe-curling sex wasn't any fun if the toes couldn't curl.

When he reached the edge of the bed and started to crawl towards me, his powerful muscles bunching under his skin, my mouth went dry. Fuck, he was gorgeous. He started to reach for the waistband of my panties but I stopped him with a shake of my head. He gave me a puzzled look.

"Take them off with your teeth."

"Fuck, woman," he muttered under his breath. "You're going to be the death of me."

"As long as you fuck me first, that's fine with me," I snapped back.

He moved up my body until we were face-to-face, his body hovering over mine, but not touching. He bent his head and I waited for him to kiss me, but he didn't. Instead, his lips traced over my jaw and then down my throat. I tilted my head back and caught a glimpse of what I hadn't seen before.

There were mirrors above the bed.

I made a mental note to decide at a later time if those were hot or creepy, and then I focused my attention on DeVon kissing his way down my body. He wasn't going so slow that we were losing momentum, but rather just slow enough to test my patience. And he was far from gentle, using his teeth until I was sure I was going to have marks all over me, but as long as he kept up that delicious pressure, I didn't care. When he finally took one of my nipples into his mouth, I gasped, my back arching as electricity shot through me.

His mouth was rougher on my nipple than it had been elsewhere. He sucked hard enough to make me cry out, then switched to the other one. My pussy throbbed and I lifted my hand to my breast. My fingers had just closed over my hardened nipple when DeVon's hand wrapped around my wrist. He looked up at me and just shook his head.

Okay, I thought. If that's how he wanted to play it. I put my hand on his head and applied a little bit of pressure, just enough for him to know that it was time to move. Something in his eyes sparked, but he let my nipple fall from his lips and ran his tongue over my stomach and down to the waistband of my panties. It wasn't until he took the material between his teeth that I realized he was actually going to do what I told him to do. With an ease that surprised me, my panties came off and disappeared over the side of the bed without ever being touched by his hands.

"You've done that before," I said.

He grinned at me as he sat back on his heels. "I've done a lot of things before, Ms. Jensen."

"So have I," I said.

He raised an eyebrow. "I may have to put that to the test."

A thrill went through me as our eyes met. He wasn't joking, and the idea excited me more than it probably should've. Something told me DeVon was the kind of man who'd test my limits and I'd beg him for more.

Without taking my eyes from his, I spread my legs and let my lips curve up into a saucy smile. "But first, why don't you put that mouth to better use?"

The corners of his mouth tightened and, for a moment, I thought he was going to balk at me telling him what to do. Then he stretched out on the bed between my legs and I shivered in antici-pation. The shiver turned into a yelp as he sank his teeth into the flesh of my inner thigh. The flash of pain quickly became absorbed into pleasure as his mouth soothed the abused skin.

He looked up. "No chance of anyone from work seeing that, is there?" The heat in his eyes said that he was only half-joking.

I wondered which part of the question's implications he was more interested in, someone from work knowing what we were doing, or anyone else being in a position to see that part of my body.

Then he was running his tongue down the length of my slit and I forgot about the question. His mouth covered me, his tongue going deep inside. I moaned, then protested when he raised his head.

"Just as you promised. Delicious." His mouth glistened as he smiled, and then he was lowering his head again.

My eyelids fluttered and I swore. Damn. He was just as good with his tongue in my pussy as he was with it in my mouth. Then he started on my clit, and I tried to lift up to get more. His hands went around my hips, holding me in place as he worked me towards climax. Wave after wave of pleasure washed over me, each one pushing me further along until I was riding the edge of an orgasm. Just as it was about to break, his mouth was gone, leaving me panting, my body a knot of frustration.

I opened my eyes, wondering if he was getting ready to fuck me, but he was just lying there, watching me. My breasts were heaving as I dragged in air and I knew my entire body was flushed. What the hell was he doing?

"Do you think you're in charge, Ms. Jensen?"

His voice was soft, almost dangerous, and I suddenly realized that I wasn't in control. Even when I'd thought I was telling him what to do, he hadn't been doing anything he hadn't wanted. He really was a control-freak.

He pushed himself up onto his knees, and I saw that he was harder than before, but he wasn't paying any attention to himself. That intense gaze was completely focused on me.

"You're not going to come until I decide to let you." He lightly ran the tip of his index finger across my sensitive flesh and I bit my lips to keep from whimpering.

Just a little more.

"*If* I decide to let you."

Fuck that.

I raised my hand to my mouth and licked my fingers. I watched his eyes follow my hand down my stomach, my destination evident. Just before I could reach what I wanted, and prove to him that I wasn't about to listen to him, his hand closed over mine. I opened my mouth to protest, but then he was dragging our hands down between my legs and my jaw snapped shut.

He pushed our fingers between my lips, rubbing my clit too hard to take me right over the edge. My body bucked, the nearly painful sensation radiating out until I thought I'd explode. I could feel myself taking this new feeling and folding it into what had been there before, building on it.

I'd always liked a little kink. Handcuffs. A little bit of hair pulling. Fucking hard and fast. This...this wasn't like anything I'd experienced before and if the pressure inside me was any indication, I liked it.

Then, just before I could come, he pulled our hands away.

"Dammit!" I cried out in pure frustration. "What the hell?"

"Do you think you're in charge?" he repeated his previous question.

I sat up and caught a look of surprise on his face. I wrapped my hand around his cock and gave it two firm strokes. He couldn't stop himself from moaning and the sound turned into a growl as I wrapped my lips around the head.

"Fuck!"

His hands found my hair as I began to lick and suck as much as I could. What I couldn't get into my mouth, I used both hands to stroke. His fingers tangled in my hair, sending little tingles of pain through my scalp and when he began to tug, I knew he was close.

Let's see how he liked it.

I released him so suddenly that his body swayed forward before he caught himself. I had a smug look on my face until I looked up at him. My mouth went dry. Oh, fuck. Maybe that hadn't been such a smart idea.

He grabbed my legs, using them to put me on my back, then spread them wide. He thrust two fingers into my pussy, causing me to cry out. He didn't even hesitate, thrusting the digits in and out as he used the heel of his palm to rub against my clit. I writhed, unsure if I was trying to get away from him or force him deeper. His free hand moved to my breast and I arched up into his touch.

I cried out as he pinched my nipple, the shock of pain twisting something deep inside me. My body began to shake, both wanting and dreading what I knew was coming. I tried to hold it back, desperate to keep his fingers inside me, keep his fingers tweaking and pulling my nipple until I exploded, but my body betrayed me and even as I started to go, his hands were gone, leaving me cursing in frustration, everything inside me screaming for release.

"Do you think you're in control, Ms. Jensen?"

"No!" I slammed my hands down on the bed. "No, you mother-fucking asshole! Now just let me come!"

"Come," he spoke the word as he leaned down and wrapped his lips around my clit.

The air rushed out of my lungs in a soundless wail as everything that had been building up came down all at once. I'd never felt anything like it before. It was like every single cell in my body had gone nuclear. My muscles clenched. My limbs spasmed. And the world went white.

I didn't know how much time passed before I started to register things around me again, but by then, I was on my stomach and I heard the sound of foil ripping.

"That, Ms. Jensen, is called edging." DeVon's voice had that sound that a man gets when he knows he's just rocked a woman's world. "And now I'm going to let you come as much as you want. I'm going to fuck you until you scream."

The arousal that had abated with my climax rushed back full force. I rolled over and pushed myself up on my hands and knees, surprised that I could even hold myself. A little voice in the back of my head was starting to protest at how much control I'd given up, but I told it to shut the hell up and looked over my shoulder at DeVon. I needed to be fucked now more than ever.

His hand was on his cock, rolling on a condom that he'd pulled from who knew where. I was just glad he had one. I'd been smart enough to bring one but I wasn't entirely sure where my purse had ended up, and I didn't want to waste time looking for it.

"Do you want me to fuck you, Ms. Jensen?"

I didn't know why he kept calling me by my last name, if it was some way to keep himself distanced from me or if it was some control thing, but I didn't care. What I did care about was getting him inside me.

"Fuck me."

He reached down and grabbed my hair, yanking on it hard enough to make me wince, but not so hard that it didn't make me even more wet, something I hadn't thought was possible. I was dripping.

"I asked for an answer to my question, not a command." His voice was harsh. "Do you want me to fuck you?"

"Yes."

"Good girl."

He kept his hand in my hair, but the other one moved between us and a moment later he was pounding into me. He didn't go slow or try to be gentle, never giving me the time to adjust to the size difference between two fingers and his cock. He took me hard and fast, each thrust making me cry out. The hand not in my hair moved underneath me to grasp one of my breasts. He teased at my nipple, pulling on it until I wasn't sure my body could handle any more conflicting sensations.

"Come for me."

The words were an order, but I was too far gone to bristle at the command. Instead, I did as I was told. He fucked me through the orgasm, despite my muscles tightening around him, and my second rolled into a third without pause. He moved his hands to my hips and my head fell forward, my hair covering my face. I could barely hold myself up and I knew if he didn't come soon, I'd start passing the point where the friction was pleasure and it would start turning to pain. His fingers dug into my flesh until I knew I'd have bruises.

"Come again for me, Krissy." His hips stuttered and I knew he was close. One hand slid around my hip to the place where our bodies joined.

Was he seriously forcing himself to hold back until I came again?

"Scream for me, baby." His fingers just barely brushed my clit and I did as he said.

I buried my face in the pillow and I screamed. He slammed into me one last time and his body stiffened, but I was barely aware of that as I rode my orgasm. I was still coming when the door banged open.

DeVon's body curved over mine as he snarled, "Doesn't anyone ever fucking knock anymore?"

FORTY-TWO

DEVON

My first instinct was to shield Krissy from whoever had come into the room, and that was enough to shock me into rolling off of her. I felt her body quiver as I slid out of her, and I vaguely wondered if she'd come again, then whoever had come in was already talking.

"When one of my staff told me someone was fucking in my bedroom, I should have known it was you, you glorified bastard."

I recognized the voice a split second before I saw the speaker. He was short and stocky, with one of those perpetually grinning faces except his wasn't fake. Steven Morrison was a genuinely good-natured kind of guy, one of the few Hollywood types I actually liked.

"Steven, love your bedroom." I didn't bother to cover up as I faced him.

"Fuck, DeVon. You are so my hero." Steven shook his head.

"I'd shake your hand, but you might not want that." I grinned at him. I half-turned, hoping Krissy had at least managed to cover up. The thought of Steven seeing her naked wasn't one I liked.

She was gone, and so was a sheet we'd somehow dislodged.

"She's a little shy." I laughed as I turned back to face Steven.

"Sounded like the two of you were going at it good. Who is she?"

I didn't even hesitate in my answer. "I don't even remember her name." I made a dismissive gesture. "Someone I picked up downstairs."

Steven laughed. "You sick fuck. Stealing my ladies." He turned towards the door, still talking. "Anyway, let's do lunch soon. There's a new project I want to show you."

"Absolutely," I said. "Let's do it next week." At least with Steven, I didn't have to fake being interested. He usually had good taste in projects.

"I'll have my assistant call yours." As he was leaving, he called over his shoulder, "And clean the fuck up after yourself."

I let out a sigh of relief as I stood. I wasn't embarrassed about being caught fucking, but I hadn't wanted Steven to know who it was. I tossed my condom into a nearby trashcan and headed to where I figured Krissy had gone. I rapped my knuckles against the door.

"Coast's clear."

The door opened and Krissy stood there with one of Steven's expensive sheets wrapped around her. Without a word, I grabbed the edges of the sheet and opened it.

"Damn, you are so fucking beautiful." I couldn't take my eyes off of her. I didn't think I could ever get tired of looking at those firm breasts with their dark nipples. They were the perfect size, and I thought if anyone ever tried to tell her to get a boob job, I'd kill them.

"You're not so bad yourself," she replied. She ran her hand down my chest and my skin burned.

When her fingers trailed below my bellybutton, I laughed and took a step back even though everything in me was cursing me for the move. "If you keep that up, we'll have to go again, and Steven might sell tickets if we keep fucking in his bed."

She gave me a smile that I couldn't read, and I found that just as hot as her body. I'd never met anyone I didn't have figured out in a few minutes. With her, I actually had to ask.

"Why'd you run away?" I kept my question light. "Are you shy?"

The look on her face said I hadn't fooled her into thinking I was curious about her being shy. Somehow, she knew that I really wanted to know if she'd hidden because she didn't want anyone to see her with me. I just hoped she didn't realize that I was starting to think it wasn't just about work.

"I left for the same reason you didn't tell Steven who I was, I suppose. Awkward office gossip and fueling all those other rumors."

She didn't have to expound for me to know that she was talking about the rumors as to why I'd hired her.

"Yeah, that's a good reason," I agreed. I didn't tell her that I was glad she'd gone because I hadn't wanted Steven to see her naked.

We were both silent for a moment. Krissy broke it just as it had gotten to that awkward point.

"I should get home."

"Oh, okay." I hid my disappointment. I didn't want her to go, or if she went, I wanted to go with her. I didn't want the night to end, but I couldn't think of a way to say that without revealing feelings I didn't really want to admit to myself.

She went into the bathroom to clean up a bit and dress. As she turned to close the door, I caught a glimpse of the hickey I'd left on the inside of her thigh and my cock twitched. I closed my eyes and ran my hands through my hair. What the hell was happening to me?

By the time she came back out, I was dressed, but still no closer to sorting through the chaos in my head. As we walked out of the room, I couldn't take my eyes off of her, and it wasn't just because I kept remembering what she looked like under that dress. It was like I was seeing her for the first time. I'd known before that she was hot, and that we verbally sparred well. I knew she had a great work ethic, and the fire inside her made her all the more appealing. Now, after what we'd done, I knew we weren't just sexually compatible. We were combustible. She wasn't some submissive who'd surrender to me without thought. She made me want to show her how good it could be, not because it made me feel powerful but because I wanted her to be trembling with pleasure, weak from the force of her orgasms. I wanted her to submit, but I wanted her to resist, too. I wanted that fire she had. She was stubborn, passionate and perfect in every way. There was no way I could let this be it. Not now.

Dammit all to hell. I was so screwed.

FORTY-THREE

KRISSY

I'd been tempted to make this call last night when I'd gotten home. Four in the morning here was seven back in New York, but it was Sunday so I knew Carrie wouldn't be up yet since it was her day off. I also didn't want to interrupt any morning 'activities' she and Gavin might've planned. I gave her until noon her time before I finally activated FaceTime and called her.

While I waited for her to answer, my fingers tapped impatiently on my thigh and I tried not to think about the dark mark I'd seen in the shower. Just the memory of DeVon's mouth on me was enough to make me wet, and I didn't want to be turned on now. I wanted to talk to my best friend about all of the confusing things going on in my head.

"Hey, what's up, Valley Girl? Miss me already?" Carrie's cheerful voice came through as her smiling face appeared on my screen.

"I fucked my boss."

Her eyes went wide and she leaned closer to the phone. "You...you did what? You had sex with DeVon Ricci?"

"Yep." I nodded. "In Steven Morrison's bed. I'm so screwed."

A puzzled expression crossed Carrie's face. "O-kay." She drew the word out. "Maybe you should start from the beginning. You had a threesome?"

"No!" I started to laugh. This was why I needed Carrie. "I guess I should start with when I kissed him. DeVon, I mean."

I told the entire story, everything from that first kiss to going to the premiere, then the after party. I didn't leave anything out, including how much I'd wanted another go when he'd pulled the sheet off of me. When I finished, she was quiet for a minute, a thoughtful expression on her face.

"I'll be honest with you," she said. "I'm not totally surprised. I could tell you were into him. You couldn't stop talking about him."

I frowned. "Really? I don't remember mentioning him at all, hardly."

"Maybe you were just too busy flirting with that young hottie at the club to remember," she teased.

I stuck my tongue out at her. "Are you going to keep making fun of me or are you going to tell me what to do here? I need my best friend's advice, not mocking."

Carrie grew serious. "You know what I've always loved about you and still do?"

"No." I wasn't sure where she was going with that question.

"That you say exactly what's on your mind. No matter how explicit. You don't hold anything back, and that's how you should move forward. Tell him how you feel."

This wasn't helping. "But I don't know how I feel." I forced myself to keep my voice down. "I wanted to fuck him to get him out of my system. It backfired."

"You mean because he's not out of your system yet?" she asked. "Damn, just how good is this guy in bed?"

"It's not funny." I scowled at her. "Yeah, he's pretty amazing, but it's not like I haven't been with some skilled lovers before.

Besides, I'm pretty sure he's going to go fuck some hot blonde tonight."

"He's so not out of your system." She ignored my glare. "You need to work on that. Either get him out of your system completely and cut him loose, or take this relationship the next step."

"Okay, so let's pretend I want to take this a step further. What's next? Look like some plastic bimbo? Get hair extensions and go blond? Buy a Bombshell bra from Victoria's Secret?" My fingers curled, digging into my leg and reminding me of what it had felt like when DeVon had made the bruises on my hips.

"No, Krissy." Carrie chuckled. "Just keep doing what you've been doing. He's obviously already into you."

"How do you know that?" I asked. "How do you know he didn't do all this just to get in my pants?"

"Weren't you wearing a dress?"

"You know what I mean."

Carrie's words turned from teasing back to the wise and thoughtful advice I'd come to expect from her. "I don't know anything for sure, but what you're going through is just one of life's challenges. You never know what you're going to get."

That wasn't what I wanted to hear.

"You have certain expectations of DeVon now because you slept together. If he doesn't live up to those expectations, you're going to resent him, even though, by your own admission, you were working to seduce him." She paused, then asked, "He never promised you anything more, did he?"

"I see where you're going," I said. "But you know me. I'm not like that. I don't give a shit. I like having sex without a commitment. Like I said, I fucked DeVon just to get him out of my mind."

"And, like you said, it backfired," she reminded me. "You still think about him."

I sighed. "You're right. I knew you'd see right through the bullshit. That's why you're a better lawyer than I ever was."

"What are you talking about?" Carrie let me change the

subject. "You're not making any sense. You were always better than me. All through college, you were higher in every class ranking. You were the smart one." Her voice took on a wistful note. "You taught me everything I know."

A lump formed in my throat. I needed to end the call before I got too homesick and decided to forget it all and catch the first plane back to New York.

"I'll talk to him," I said.

"Don't put it off," she said. "You'll regret it."

Again, she was right. I knew that ignoring him and just waiting for the next impulsive encounter was going to be agonizing. Better to bite the bullet. We said our good-byes and I was left staring at my phone with Carrie's words echoing in my mind.

What the hell.

I flipped through my contacts until I reached his name and pressed connect before I could talk myself out of it.

"DeVon."

My insides squirmed. "Ready for round two?"

FORTY-FOUR

KRISSY

I still wasn't entirely sure how I felt about the way things were going. DeVon had indeed wanted a second go, but he'd surprised me by asking me out on a date.

Well, *asked* might not have been the most accurate word. It was more like he'd told me that before we fucked, we were going out on a date. And then he'd proceeded to tell me what to wear, down to the color of my panties. I'd considered telling him exactly what he could do with his own panties, but the memory of how hard I'd come was still fresh in my mind...as well as other places.

Besides, I'd told myself, maybe this would be what I'd need to get him out of my head. I'd see how he was outside of work, but also outside of the bedroom. I'd see the kind of person he'd be to have a relationship with and that would be enough. Not that I wanted one, but it was still a good thing to know. After tonight, whenever I found myself thinking about him, I'd remember him basically commanding me to wear a strapless dress with a long skirt but a high slit, and one that allowed me to go without a bra. My panties were to be sheer and match the dress. He wanted scarlet.

Not red, not crimson, but scarlet. Which, of course, had meant I'd had to go shopping again. This one, however, I wouldn't be able to claim as a business expense.

He damn well better make tonight worth it.

He'd sent a car to come get me, so when I walked into the restaurant, he was already waiting. I was pretty sure he'd purposefully gotten there ahead of me so he could watch me walking towards him, so I made sure he had time to enjoy it. Judging by the way his eyes darkened, he did.

He stood when I was just a couple feet away and pulled out my chair. Based on his previous behavior, that gesture should've surprised me, but it didn't. That had seemed completely natural.

"You look absolutely breath-taking," he said as he pushed the chair in. He leaned down so that his mouth was next to my ear. "As I knew you would." His breath was warm on my skin and I had to suppress a shiver even though his words were innocent.

He took a seat next to me and poured some champagne into our glasses. I wondered if he'd been here long enough to have ordered it, or if he'd told them to have it ready when the car was scheduled to arrive. I was willing to bet the latter. I looked around for a menu.

"I've already ordered."

My eyes narrowed. "Excuse me?"

DeVon seemed more amused by my reaction than anything else and that just annoyed me more. "I ordered for us when I reserved the table."

"And what if I wanted something else?" I asked.

He raised an eyebrow and took a sip of champagne "How do you know you want something else if you don't know what I ordered?"

I scowled. "That's not the point."

He gave a little shrug that seemed to say he didn't particularly care about what the point was, then he put down his glass. "Do you think you're in charge here, Ms. Jensen?"

That question sent a bolt of desire straight through me but I pushed it down.

"Why'd you do that?" I asked. "Last night, why did you call me 'Ms. Jensen' instead of Krissy?"

He faltered. I couldn't say how, exactly, but I saw it.

"Fine," he said, his tone becoming harder. "Krissy, then. The question still is, do you think you're in charge?"

I leaned forward, positioning myself to display the tops of my breasts to their best advantage. I had to admit, I did love the dress I'd found, and I looked damn good in scarlet. "I know you think you're in charge, Mr. Ricci, but I intend to show you just how wrong you are." I took a drink, proud of myself.

"Show me your panties."

I almost choked on my mouthful of champagne. He waited patiently until I'd swallowed and determined that I wasn't about to have a coughing fit, then he repeated himself with a clarification.

"If you're so adamant that I'm not in control, then show me that you disobeyed my orders and your panties aren't sheer scarlet lace."

Damn him.

My face flamed. "That's not the point."

He smiled that infuriating grin he had when something went his way. "And I'm not asking."

My temper flared, and I was torn between the desire to show of my stubborn streak and not let him anywhere near my panties, and the sexual part of me that wanted to do everything he said...with my own little twist designed to drive him crazy. Not surprisingly, my sexual side won.

We were at a private table near the back – intentionally, I had no doubt – so I could turn towards him and unless someone chose that moment to walk by, I wasn't in danger of flashing anyone but my intended target. I shifted in my seat, the movement drawing his attention down. I'd bought a dress with a high slit, just like he'd said and it allowed me enough freedom to part my knees and give DeVon a glimpse of the side of my panties, enough that he could see the color. Instead, I raised the fabric enough to let him get a good, long look at the crotch of the nearly see-through panties I'd just purchased.

The hand on the table curled into a fist and I knew the game was on. It would be back and forth all night to see which one of us cracked first. For the first time in my life, however, I wasn't entirely sure that it wouldn't be me.

We made small talk as the appetizers arrived and then the next round began. I'd learned fairly young into my sexual years that anything that drew attention to the mouth and could make a guy think about you sucking his cock was a surefire way to get his attention. I'd perfected the art and knew exactly how to use my lips and tongue to keep a man's mind exactly where I wanted it.

What I hadn't expected was that, with the right mouth, a man could do the same thing.

By the time our main course was coming to its end, I was starting to wonder if I was in over my head. I'd met guys with big attitudes, and had fucked plenty who'd thought they were the best thing to happen to women since AA batteries, but I'd never met someone who played the game like DeVon.

As he licked the crumbs from his lips, DeVon leaned towards me and I found myself tensing in anticipation.

"Take them off."

I blinked. What was he talking about?

"Your panties. Take them off."

I shook my head, a smile playing on my lips. "I don't think so. You take yours off."

He dropped his voice, the corner of his mouth twitching in amusement. "Who said I was wearing any?"

I stared at him for a moment. I told myself that I should be annoyed that he assumed I'd be okay with what he was telling me to do, but all I could think about was reaching over, unzipping his pants and having nothing between my hand and his cock.

"Take them off." There was a warning in his tone that hadn't been there before. "There will be consequences if you refuse."

Okay, now I was going to say no just to find out what he was going to do. I drained the last of my champagne and gave him a look that clearly said I wasn't going to do shit.

He stood and moved his chair over so that we were sitting next to each other. He didn't say anything as he sat back down, and then I felt his hand brush against my leg. I tensed, but his fingers slid further under the slit of my dress. I thought about closing my legs as his palm skimmed over my thigh, but I resisted. There was no way he was going to do what he wanted me to think he was going to do.

His fingers skimmed the crotch of my panties and I sucked in a breath. He chuckled and I gritted my teeth. There was no way in hell I was going to blink first. He'd stop before I broke.

"For tonight," he said in a conversational tone. "This is mine." His index finger slipped beneath the damp fabric. The tip caressed my lips, then delved between them, going straight for my core. "And nothing comes between me and what's mine."

A second finger joined the first and I had to grab the edge of the table to keep from doing something stupid like slapping him...or possibly grabbing his cock. His fingers moved rapidly in and out of my pussy as he kept talking.

"I'll make you come so hard you see stars. I'll fuck you until every man after me will only be second best. I'll give you great pleasure, Krissy."

Suddenly, he shoved a third finger into me, and I gasped as he pushed them deep.

"But do not ever think that refusing to obey comes without consequences." He paused, then spoke again, the tone of his voice changing to sound completely normal. "I believe we will have some dessert."

I looked up, my heart leaping into my throat as I realized the waiter was standing in front of us, and DeVon was carrying on a conversation as if he didn't have three fingers buried in my pussy.

"The fresh strawberries and cream will be perfect."

"I'll be right back." The waiter smiled at us both, and I wondered if he realized that something was going on.

DeVon pulled out his fingers so quickly that I had to bite my lip to keep from crying out. My body protested, wanting me to beg him to finish what he'd started. I didn't care that we were in a restaurant. I just needed him to stop the ache inside me. My hands curled into fists, nails biting into my palms. Oh, I was definitely losing the game, but I had a feeling I was still going to like how it ended.

"Now." He stood. "I'm going to the restroom to wash my hands. When I come back, you will have done as you were told, or we will see if I can't find a more...persuasive way of convincing you that obedience is in your best interest."

FORTY-FIVE

DEVON

When we left the restaurant, Krissy's panties were in my jacket pocket, and I knew that we were going to have one hell of a night. Oh, she continued to test me, but that was part of what made our dance so hot. She wasn't like the women who made scenes or deliberately disobeyed because they craved pain and humiliation. No, Krissy understood the power of words. I could see now how talented a lawyer she was. As I drove us back to my place in silence, I couldn't help but imagine what it would be like to see her in a courtroom, holding a jury in the palm of her hand...and then bending her over the railing and taking her.

I glanced over at her and saw that she was watching me, a thoughtful expression on her face. I'd been very careful not to touch her since she'd given me her panties and I could tell she was wondering why. Part of it was because I wanted her to crave my touch. If I didn't give it to her, she would want it more. Another part, a new part, was that I didn't entirely trust myself. The feel and scent of her skin was intoxicating and I wasn't sure I could make tonight into what I wanted if I kept physical contact. A quickie in the car might be fun, but I had much more interesting things planned.

We stepped onto the elevator ten minutes later and as soon as the doors closed, Krissy was in front of me, her hands on my chest, pushing me back against the wall. Her eyes locked with mine and she dropped her hand, cupping me through my pants.

"I was beginning to think you weren't interested," she said, giving me a light squeeze.

I grabbed her wrist and turned us so that she was the one against the wall. I put her arm above her head and pushed aside her dress to get my hand between her legs. Fuck, she was wet. She moaned as my fingers rubbed over her clit.

"Did I say you could touch me?" My face was less than an inch from hers, and I wanted to close that gap and kiss her, but I restrained myself.

"I figured if mine was yours, yours must be mine." The words were punctuated with little gasps of pleasure.

The elevator dinged and I knew it was too soon for my penthouse. I didn't move, but I saw Krissy's eyes dart over my shoulder, then widen. She struggled against me and I knew someone was standing there.

"Take the next one," I barked, releasing Krissy's wrist long enough to reach behind me and hit the close doors button. I didn't wait for them to finish closing before I began to rub her clit again. "Come for me."

She shook her head, her face flushing. "Not here."

"Yes, here," I insisted. "You started this. You wanted to get me worked up in the elevator. Now the tables are turned." I pinched her nipple through the soft fabric of her dress. "Come for me, or we'll ride this elevator until you do. And next time, I won't tell anyone to wait for another one."

A shiver went through her, and I knew she was close.

"Is that what you want?" I asked. "Do you want to climax in

front of people?" I put my mouth against her ear. "Come for me, Krissy, or you're going to find out."

A soft exhalation escaped her lips and I felt her body tense. I removed my hand from between her legs, and held her fingers to her lips. Her eyes flashed and, for a moment, I thought she'd argue, but instead, she opened her mouth and licked my fingers clean.

I was about to burst by the time we reached my floor.

"I have to ask." Krissy broke the silence as I unlocked the door. "What's with the apartment? Don't you have a fabulous house? Or is this just the place you bring women to fuck?"

"I don't always feel like driving back to my house if I've been working late," I explained. "Or if I've been at a premiere or party or something like that." I gave her a heated look before stepping inside. "Or if I don't want to wait any extra time when I'm with a beautiful woman."

I took off my shoes, jacket and tie, tossing the last two onto my expensive antique dining room table. If we'd been dating for real, I might've felt compelled to show her around the place, let her see the excellent job Donna, my interior designer, had done, but we weren't a couple, even if we had just gone to dinner.

I turned around and found that she'd taken off her shoes. I'd forgotten that she was actually just a bit above average height without her heels. I looked down at her and began to slowly unbutton my shirt. When I was halfway down, I turned around and started towards the bedroom.

I didn't even glance back to see if she was following. I knew she was. Like at my house, I had two bedrooms here for two different purposes. I had the one where I slept and the one where I fucked, some because I didn't always feel like changing the sheets in the middle of the night and some because I didn't do the whole afterwards cuddle thing.

The bedroom was tastefully done, but catered to my sexual preferences. The bed was large, and had both a headboard and posts at the base that were used for bondage. I had a dresser with a few toys and a flogger. My collection here was nowhere near what I had at my house, but it was enough for what I wanted to do most of the time.

As my shirt fell to the floor, a pair of arms slid around my waist, and Krissy pressed her body against mine. Her hands went to the button and zipper at the front of my pants and my lips twitched in a smile. I'd been hoping she was going to keep pushing back. I loved the give and take with her, and right now, I was really looking forward to giving.

As soon as her hands managed to get the zipper partway down, I wrapped my fingers around her wrists, preventing her from going any further. I twisted us around so that she was facing me, her hands held against my bare chest.

"Someone has wandering hands." I used my free hand to reach into the top drawer of the dresser. I considered handcuffs, but I wasn't sure how she'd take that since we hadn't discussed bondage, so I went with something just as restrictive, but a little less scary.

The strip of cotton was soft enough that it wouldn't cut her like silk, but strong enough that it'd keep her restrained, which was what I wanted. It also gave me a bit more flexibility on positioning her. As I tied her wrists, I waited for her to protest, but she didn't. Instead, she just watched with a smug little smirk on her face.

When I finished, she finally spoke, "So is this my punishment for doing what you told me not to?"

I wrapped my arm around her waist. "No." I pulled her with me as I sat on the bed. "This is." I turned her over my knee, enjoying the shocked expression on her face before she began to struggle.

"Cut it out, DeVon." She sounded annoyed.

I ran my finger down her spine and she shivered. "Struggle and protest all you want. If you truly want me to stop, just say 'red' and we're done." I reached down to her face and ran my thumb across her bottom lip. "But understand this. If you say it, we're done. We don't come back here again. We work together and that's it."

I slid my hand across her back and down over the swell of her ass as I watched her think. Her muscles tensed as my hand moved over her firm flesh, but I didn't do anything. I needed her to agree first. I liked control and I'd push the limits, but I had never forced myself on anyone and never would. They always agreed.

My fingers found the slit in the dress and brushed against her bare skin. She nodded.

My hand came down on her ass with a stinging slap. Instinctively, she started to squirm, causing almost painful friction against my cock. I spanked her again, hard enough to feel, but not even close to as hard as I'd done to other women. I wanted to feel her flesh warm against my palm, so I pulled the skirt of her dress aside. Definitely one of the many reasons I liked long dresses with high slits.

"You have a gorgeous ass," I said as I left a red mark on her skin. My hand began to burn and somewhere between the fourth and fifth blow, Krissy's little yelps of pain became mixed with moans of pleasure.

"Do you like this?" I asked.

"Fuck you." Her voice was shaking, and I recognized the sound I'd heard many times before. She wanted this, but couldn't admit it. She thought it made her weak. I may have been the one in control, but the women who wanted what I had to offer were never weak.

I slid my hand down between her legs and found her dripping. I pushed a finger inside her and she groaned. "That answers my question."

I scooped her up and tossed her on the bed. I heard her suck in air as her ass slid over the sheets. I pulled off my pants, sighing in relief as my cock was finally free of its constraints. Krissy glared up at me as I climbed onto the bed. Good. She hadn't lost her fire.

"You don't play fair," she said as I reached for the side zipper of her dress.

"You have no idea." I slowly peeled off the clingy fabric, taking the time to enjoy the way her body was revealed inch by inch.

"You knew you were going to do this." Her voice took on an accusing tone. "That's why you had me get a strapless dress."

I tossed it onto the floor. "It was either that, or I'd have to cut it off of you, and while I liked that idea, I didn't think it would be fair to you to destroy a dress you'd paid for."

She stared up at me, lips parted in shock. I took advantage and covered her mouth with mine, shoving my tongue into her mouth. I took my time exploring, tasting the strawberries, cream and champagne we'd shared. And, of course, the flavor of her from when she'd cleaned my fingers in the elevator. It was a heady combination.

When I straightened, her eyes were glassy, her magnificent breasts heaving as she caught her breath. My own heart was racing as I raised her bound hands above her head. I'd ordered this headboard specially made with elaborate metalwork. The thing that made it special was that the designs had been specifically created to hide their true purpose, allowing them to be both decorative and useful. The cotton strip around her wrist slipped easily over the curved metal, effectively tethering her to the headboard without needing to tie anything. It was complex enough that she most likely wouldn't pull free during sex, but not so much that she couldn't get out of it if she truly wanted to.

"You said I wasn't playing fair, and yet you've been working just as hard to undermine me." I cupped her breasts, one in either hand. "I should teach you a lesson, tease you to the point of orgasm over and over again until you truly understand what it means to burn with need. You've experienced only a small part of that. Imagine what it would be like for hours."

She whimpered as I rolled her hardening nipples between my thumbs and forefingers, and I could see she despised herself for it. Along with that, however, I saw her fear that I would do just as I'd said, torture her with denial.

"I'm not going to do that," I said. The relief that washed over her was evident. "I'm going to allow you to come as often as you can, but it's not a reward." I leaned down and flicked my tongue over one nipple, then the other. I kissed my way up her chest to her throat, stopping by her ear. "I love the way you look when you come." Her body twisted as I sucked her earlobe into my mouth, lightly biting down on it.

I slid my body down hers, keeping only the lightest contact until I settled between her legs. She spread them willingly, and if I hadn't been focusing on the glistening folds in front of me, I might've smirked. Instead, I wrapped my hands around her hips and plunged my tongue inside her.

Krissy let out a wordless cry and her back arched. Fuck, I loved that sound. Nothing was as hot as hearing a woman calling out in pleasure, and being the one who made it happen. The fact that she was Krissy made it even that much hotter. I circled her clit with my tongue, then took it into my mouth. I wanted to hear her scream.

When she came, I kept sucking on that little bundle of nerves, wanting to drive her further and further up, almost to the point of pain. She made a sound like a half-sob when I finally released her clit, but I didn't completely back off. I went to work below. I wasn't one of those men who performed oral sex in hopes of getting a return favor, or even just as foreplay to make sure the girl was wet enough, or even the ones who did it because they couldn't get their partner off any other way. I actually enjoyed it, and with Krissy, even more than usual. I knew that meant I was getting myself in deeper than I wanted to, but I didn't care at the moment. I could worry about that later. All that mattered was that she was starting to build up towards another orgasm and I was determined to get her there before I fucked her.

"Shit, shit, shit!!"

The last word turned into a wail as her pussy spasmed around my tongue. I kept working at her until she was as far as she could go, and then I pushed myself onto my knees. I'd had this room designed so that everything I needed was within arm's reach. That meant before Krissy had even started coming down from her high, I had a condom on and was sliding inside her still quivering pussy.

"Fuck," I groaned. I squeezed my eyes shut and tried not to embarrass myself. It wasn't easy, but I finally gained enough control to drive myself deeper. We fit together so perfectly. I didn't know how I was going to be able to give this up.

FORTY-SIX

KRISSY

I didn't know what the fuck I was doing. The little dance DeVon and I had been doing at the restaurant hadn't really pissed me off like I'd thought it would. I liked being in charge, and I'd never liked being told what to do, even when I'd been a kid, but there was something about DeVon that made dark things deep inside me twist and squirm. At first, I'd thought it was just his raw sexuality – the man basically breathed sex – but when he'd started fingering me in the elevator, I'd had to admit that a part of me found it hot. Still, I'd had to tease him, had to remind him that I wasn't some needy little submissive.

Then things had taken a turn I hadn't been expecting. I wasn't sure which part shocked me more, that he'd turned me over his knee, that I hadn't taken the out he'd given me, or that after the initial sting, I'd actually started to like it. It hadn't hurt, not really, though I suspected he could've kept going until it did. As the heat had bloomed across my skin, it had gone down to my pussy, and I hadn't been able to deny my arousal when he'd put his finger inside me.

Now, my wrists were chafed and aching as I tugged at the headboard, desperate to regain some sort of control after being helpless under the assault of his mouth. As he thrust into me, I wanted to have my hands on him, drag my nails over his skin, dig them into his back, into that firm ass. I'd never realized how much I'd used my hands for an outlet during sex and I couldn't now. Everything was focused on the feeling of him stretching me, filling me, over and over. Each stroke rubbed him against my g-spot until I was seeing sparks. The tension inside me was unbearable and I knew I was going to come again. Two was usually a good fuck for me, three if I helped the guy along. But DeVon always defied the odds. Right now, I was on number four and he wasn't showing any sign of slowing.

I screamed as I came, needing to release the pressure as my body shook. He kept going and leaned down, scraping his teeth over my nipple and sending another rush of pleasure through me. My eyes rolled and I stopped trying to get free. I gasped for air, my body telling me it'd had enough, and then, suddenly, he was gone, leaving me empty.

"My turn."

I forced my eyes to focus. DeVon was kneeling directly in front of me, his knees on either side of my shoulders, his cock hard and glistening.

"Open."

My muddled brain didn't even try to protest. I opened my mouth and he slid his cock between my lips. Tied down without use of my hands meant I had to trust him as he began to slowly thrust. He kept them shallow, but I could see the struggle on his face. He wanted to fuck my mouth, and a part of me I'd never acknowledged before said that it wanted him to. This wasn't the time, though. I didn't trust him *that* much. I focused on the few inches in my mouth, swirling my tongue around it, tasting myself and him mingled together. When I hollowed out my cheeks, sucking hard on the firm flesh, he swore and pulled out.

He unhooked my hands from the headboard and buried his fingers in my hair, pulling me up until he could crush his mouth against mine. He put my still-bound hands around his neck as he bit and sucked on my lips and tongue. He lifted me, wrapping my legs around his waist. The kiss set my nerves on fire so that as I sank down onto him, I came again, my pussy squeezing his cock so tightly that his fingers dug into my ass.

He lifted me until just the tip remained inside, then dropped me, letting gravity do the work. I swore as the movement drove him deeper inside me than he'd been before. He repeated it, only this time, he thrust up as I was coming down and I wailed. As he slammed into me, I danced that fine line between pleasure and pain. My brain and body didn't know how to translate the signals coming from every single nerve-ending. I clung to him as he fucked me, not sure if I wanted to beg him to stop or tell him to never stop. My pussy throbbed. My ass burned. My clit rubbed against the base of his cock until I was sure it was raw and swollen.

"Please, Krissy."

I could feel the difference in his movements, the urgency as he pounded into me, and I knew he was close. I shifted my weight, the movement throwing him enough off-balance that we fell backwards, him onto his back and me on top of him. I dropped onto him and everything exploded in a burst of pain and ecstasy so intense that I almost missed him calling out my name as he came.

I fell forward onto him and his arms wrapped around me, holding me as our bodies shuddered and trembled together.

I didn't even know I'd passed out until I was opening my eyes, and that was when I realized that DeVon's body was curled around mine, and we were both wrapped in a sheet. His breathing told me he wasn't sleeping, and as soon as I shifted, he let me go and pushed himself up into a sitting position.

I didn't look at him as I sat up, grimacing as my ass rubbed against the sheets. Dammit. I hoped that'd be better by tomorrow or work was going to be hell. I didn't say anything as I climbed off of the bed and headed for the bathroom. What was I supposed to say after that? Thanks for the mind-blowing orgasms? Thanks for spanking me? How the hell was I supposed to know what to say if I couldn't even begin to wrap my mind around how I felt about what had happened?

When I stepped back into the bedroom, ready for an awkward conversation, DeVon was standing there with his pants on and my clothes neatly piled on the bed. Surprisingly, he kept his eyes on my face as I walked over to retrieve my clothing.

"You can sleep in here, if you'd like, or I can call the car service to take you home." His voice was carefully neutral, as if he didn't want me to know which option he was hoping I'd take.

I wasn't going to worry about that. I had enough of my own shit to sort through now without worrying about trying to read him. "I'll just catch a taxi. I'm sure there are plenty around here."

He nodded, opened his mouth, then closed it again.

"Spit it out," I said as I zipped up my dress.

"I don't want this to come out the wrong way," he started.

I motioned for him to continue, curious now as to what he could possibly want to say that could come across wrong.

"Do you need cab fare?"

I grinned. "What self-respecting New York woman goes out on a date without cab fare for a late-night ride home?"

He laughed, and the tension that had threatened to grow eased instead. My head was still chaotic, but at least things between DeVon and I weren't weird. He walked me to the door, but didn't try to kiss me good-bye. Part of me wished he had, but I understood why he hadn't. We weren't in a relationship.

And it was okay, because it *had* to be okay.

"I'll see you tomorrow," I said as I headed for the elevator. I might freak out later, and I knew I'd definitely be trying to examine everything at some point, but for tonight, I was going to accept that I'd had fun with someone I found insanely attractive, and who I actually liked spending time with too.

And I refused to let fear ruin the good thing we had going.

THE END

Krissy's story continues in *Craving Perfection (Club Prive Book 4)*, available now.

ABOUT THE AUTHOR

M. S. Parker is a USA Today Bestselling author and the author of the Erotic Romance series, Club Privè and Chasing Perfection.

Living in Las Vegas, she enjoys sitting by the pool with her laptop writing on her next spicy romance.

Growing up all she wanted to be was a dancer, actor or author. So far only the latter has come true but M. S. Parker hasn't retired her dancing shoes just yet. She is still waiting for the call for her to appear on Dancing With The Stars.

When M. S. isn't writing, she can usually be found reading– oops, scratch that! She is always writing.

For more information:
www.msparker.com
msparkerbooks@gmail.com

 facebook.com/msparkerauthor

ACKNOWLEDGMENTS

First, I would like to thank all of my readers. Without you, my books would not exist. I truly appreciate each and every one of you.

A big "thanks" goes out to all the Facebook fans, street team, beta readers, and advanced reviewers. You are a HUGE part of the success of all my series.

I have to thank my PA, Shannon Hunt. Without you my life would be a complete and utter mess. Also a big thank you goes out to my editor Lynette and my wonderful cover designer, Sinisa. You make my ideas and writing look so good.